CHAFF ON THE *Wind*

BRENDA K. SAVELLA

CHAFF ON THE WIND

Printed in Canada

ISBN: 978-1-4866-2522-2
eBook ISBN: 978-1-4866-2523-9

Word Alive Press
119 De Baets Street Winnipeg, MB R2J 3R9
www.wordalivepress.ca

Cataloguing in Publication information can be obtained from Library and Archives Canada.

For Francis John, my dearest friend always.

As a pastor, God places on our journey angels in our midst. For myself, Brenda was one of these angels who stepped forward to preside in the pulpit in my absence. She did so ever so humbly and yet so capably. I perceive Brenda as one who is following in her Master's footsteps, as she has been blessed with a sense of the holy and with a delivery which is so down to earth. She is gentle and easy to listen to. She does not come across as judgemental but rather as one filled with a spirit of grace. Prayers whisper forth in the midst of her presence. I believe readers will find in Brenda such a sincere interest for others to experience His presence of peace and acceptance.

—Rev. John Burrill

Let them be like chaff before the wind,
with the angel of the Lord driving them on.
—Psalm 35:5

ACKNOWLEDGEMENTS

A little chickadee sat on the fence beside me chirping softly as I enjoyed a sunny morning last spring. Later that week, I realized it had come to bring me great news. My book was a finalist for the 2023 Braun Book Award for fiction. It was one of the great joys of my life. Thank you, Word Alive Press, for sponsoring the award!

I want to acknowledge my beautiful sister, Colleen Hayward, who told me that I could write a great book. I just had to try. Thanks for your belief in me. I love you always.

Francis John, you have been the best friend a girl could have. You were expecting the next great Canadian novel from me; I'll keep trying for you. Thanks for the continuous encouragement throughout the years. You laid down your life for me in so many beautiful ways so that I could accomplish what I couldn't have done without you.

My deepest and heartfelt thanks to Evan Braun, inspired wordsmith and editor. You know how to make just the right comments and ask the perfect questions. I learned so much from you! Somehow thank you doesn't seem enough.

To my two project managers, Crystal Hildebrandt and Ariana Forsman. Crystal, you offered encouragement and guidance through the initial paces of book publishing. Thank you for your patience and your wise, gentle spirit. When you said, "Brenda, your book is beautiful," it gave me the courage to pursue this journey. Ariana, you brought me through the last leg of this journey. I so appreciate your knowledge, skill, kindness, and patience. Thank you, ladies!

Thank you to the production team at Word Alive Press. From the cover design to final page design, and throughout the whole publishing process, you did a wonderful job. Thanks to everyone for putting up with my weak technological skills while I learned to use the correct software!

A warm thank you to Chantal Dorais at Edmonton Public Library who provided invaluable computer software assistance with good humour. High five to you, Chantal!

Special thanks to everyone who buys this book. I hope that it touches your life and helps you to dream big dreams or recover those you lost along life's way. May your own creative pilgrimage touch others in a positive way.

To God be the glory.

One

Edmonton, Alberta
August 1996

The chickadee's call against the early dawn permeated the corn-silk-coloured room through the lifted screen of the balcony door. Annabel Adams rolled onto her side and groaned. The repetitive bird sounds punctuated every fibre of her being like minute stabs, even though she generally considered birdsong to be melodic, even soothing.

"It's worse than an alarm clock!"

She muttered it quietly enough not to awaken her husband, who slept soundly beside her. His soft snore added to the unwelcome noise. Everything seemed to bother her these days, and this morning it went way beyond irritation; sound itself seemed unbearable. Her friend Nora had said it was her sensitive artistic nature that caused the problem, a highly sensitive nervous system that was overwrought.

It's not as though I've been doing anything with that artistic nature, she argued to herself. *Conner doesn't approve of my artistic inclinations. He says I have to get a real job, not think that I can just stay home and paint. I have to be a viable financial contributor. But given time and emotional support, I could become one through my art.*

Annabel hiked herself up and bunched up the three pillows behind her so she could lean against them. Weariness pressed in upon her. It was so unfair. A gal was supposed to feel rested after a night's sleep, not be more tired than she had been when she went to bed. It wasn't as if she had to go to work each day anymore. She had the summer off from her last meaningless job, the one she'd held before being accepted to graduate school for the fall.

Graduate school. A master's degree in counselling psychology, with the hope of becoming a chartered psychologist one day. It was a new path, albeit one that would probably lead her even farther away from producing art.

Yet it seemed to be a plan that Conner approved of, and wasn't every good Christian wife supposed to please her husband? She would add to the family finances and make him happy.

She sighed deeply.

Glancing at the back of his head, she studied the hills and valleys of Conner's dark curls. His hair was shiny and finely textured. For a moment, she found herself wanting to run her fingers through it, lifting the strands to catch the first rays of sunlight, but it seemed like too much effort. Instead she stared out the window to watch the bands of pink and yellow above the horizon dissolve slowly into the growing expanse of blue.

It was early Saturday morning and already warm enough to predict another hot, dry August day in Edmonton. There wasn't a cloud in the sky and the only way to cope with the heat in an old house like this was to leave the second-floor balcony door open and the screen window up all night.

Annabel pushed herself up with both hands and dangled her feet off the side of the bed. Barely five feet three inches, she sometimes felt like a child climbing out of the old-fashioned brass-canopied bed. At thirty-nine, she still looked young, but childhood was far behind her. Probably even childbearing, but that was just another irritating issue.

She slid down the few inches and reached her toes to the hardwood floor.

"What's up, sunshine?" Conner's voice was soft and husky. He rolled to face her, leaning his elbow on the pillow so he could support his head with his right hand. His long torso, shirtless above the lightweight sheet, was moist with light perspiration.

"Nothing," she replied.

"You're up early."

"Yes, and as tired as though I hadn't slept at all."

There was agitation in her voice even though she hadn't meant to sound upset. She sighed again and walked toward the door. It had been the same thing for months, maybe even years. Didn't he already know what was up?

Annabel pushed the door fully open and stepped out onto the grey-carpeted balcony before she let it snap shut.

"Perhaps you should put a robe on," Conner suggested softly.

"It's not even six o'clock on a Saturday morning. Only the birds and us are up. Besides, my pyjamas aren't see-through."

The disagreeable tone remained in her voice. She moved to the left out of his view and sat on one of the wrought iron chairs. With both elbows on the table, she cupped her face in her hands. She wanted to scream or cry, or both. She hoped Conner stayed inside and gave her this moment of quiet, yet she would feel equally let down if he didn't come to her.

She waited and sighed again when she heard the door click open.

"Can I get you anything, sunshine?"

"No. I'm okay. Go back to bed and get some more rest. I'll just sit here quietly among the tree branches and leaves."

The tears were about to start again, but she willed herself not to cry. What in the world was the matter with her anyway? There was a restless, oppressive feeling she just couldn't seem to shake off. Even prayer didn't seem to lift it.

Conner wanted to help but didn't know what to do. He leaned against the doorframe watching his petite wife stare mindlessly straight ahead.

"How about getting breakfast somewhere?" he suggested. "That little French bakery has great chocolate croissants. And tea is still the best drink of the day."

She turned and glanced up at him, then shook her head without a word.

Conner waited. He desperately wanted to say something that would make things better. It was true that he had been busy at work, and perhaps he had inadvertently been neglectful of his wife. His mind quickly went over some possibilities.

"Look, sunshine, maybe a trip to the mountains would help. You always say that the mountain air does wonders for you."

His voice was tentative. She could tell he didn't want to say the wrong thing and set her off on a bad track for the day. And it did seem that she was spending more and more time on the wrong track. The ruts were deep and she could feel herself carried along in a direction that didn't seem to benefit either of them.

"You said you couldn't take time off right now," she said. "Remember?"

"No, I can't, but that doesn't mean you can't go by yourself. Take the dog and head up to Banff. You could stay in a hotel and just have some time to yourself. Maybe that would help."

"There's only one place in Banff that takes animals, and I don't like it." She turned toward him and looked upward, thinking for a few moments. When she continued, there was a hint of enthusiasm. "But I could camp, couldn't I?"

"I don't like the idea of you camping alone." He already regretted his suggestion, but he tried to keep his voice level. "How would you set the tent up by yourself? I've done it the few times we've camped, and I've always done it by myself."

"Not because I didn't want to help. You wouldn't let me. You could show me how to put up the tent. Conner, I could take my journal, and maybe a sketchbook. I could manage."

She looked up into his handsome face. His eyebrows, now drawn together, formed a stern expression. He was biting on his lower lip.

But the idea had taken hold of her. It had been a while since she'd felt much real interest in anything, and camping in the mountains was beginning to feel like an adventure. The mountains always made her feel closer to God; that was something she needed.

"I'm worried that you're too vulnerable right now," he said. "There aren't any locks on tent doors, you know."

"Yes, I am aware of that. But I would be really careful. I promise. Besides, I'll have Muffin with me. She'd bark up a storm if anyone tried to come near."

"I don't know about that. I'm not sure I trust her judgment. She's friendly with everyone, even though Lhasa Apsos are supposed to be more discerning."

"Well, I trust her. Please, Conner, I believe you're right. This is what I need. You could show me how to set up the tent today. I'll practice. We could go buy food this afternoon. It won't take me long to pack. I just need jeans and walking shorts, T-shirts, a sweater, and a jacket."

"Don't forget it gets really cold up in the mountains, even in summer."

"I'll take my portable cot, sleeping bag, woollen blanket, even extra blankets. A thick woollen sweater. The small electric kettle. There are outlets in the campground washrooms. That way, I can have hot tea every morning right at the campsite without a stove." She added sheepishly, "Sort of afraid of propane stoves, remember? I'll stick to soup cups, sandwiches, fruit, yogurt… things I don't have to cook."

For the first time in many weeks, a slight smile curved the corners of her mouth. There was a spark of light in her eyes again. The mountains had a healing quality. Annabel was certain of it. This was the answer she needed.

Conner dropped his head, feeling resigned. He had no choice; he had to let her go. "Okay. How long do you want to go for?"

"What about a week?"

Conner shook his head slightly as he lifted his shoulders in a shrug. He knew he was beaten. After all, Banff had been his idea in the first place. He didn't know why he even suggested it.

He let a puff of air escape noisily from between his pursed lips. He missed the woman with whom he had first fallen in love. The carefree Annabel who had been so much fun. She seemed to have slipped away over the past few years, but he hadn't been able to figure out why. Maybe this brief time apart would give her time to think, time to find herself again.

"Can we try out the tent now?" she pleaded, her green eyes widened with blooming excitement. "That way I can leave tomorrow morning. People usually end their vacations on Sundays, don't they? I'm sure to get a good camping spot."

It was early, but Conner knew it was best just to give in. He nodded and went inside the house.

A few minutes later, she could hear the taps running in the bathroom. Slowly she rose, stretched her arms overhead, and yawned. Hope was percolating inside and she felt a prayer rise from a deep place in her spirit.

Let this be what I need, dear Lord. Help me to understand what in the world is wrong with me. Let me be able to get back on the right track. Refresh me through this adventure. Let it breathe new life into me. Amen.

Yes, hope was certainly arising.

Two

Sunday morning came quickly for Annabel. At five o'clock, she crept downstairs to the tiny kitchen and put the copper kettle onto the small electric stove to boil water for tea.

She sat at the white drop-leaf table by the window contemplating her life. Never before had she felt so out of sorts. Life no longer seemed to make much sense. Marriage was supposed to bring fulfillment, wasn't it? Yet she felt anything but fulfilled; in fact, she felt disconnected. And as for her work life, she hadn't found anything satisfying for the long term. Hopefully, that would change in the fall when she started her training. Maybe helping to counsel others through their difficulties would be easier than trying to figure out her own life.

She had attached so much guilt to her life as it was. With her religious upbringing and personal faith, life was supposed to be more meaningful. She had to be doing something wrong. Why didn't she seem to feel much joy in life anymore? Conner was often busy with his career in academic research and tended to work late, giving her more time to herself. Maybe too much time. Time she did nothing with even though she kept promising herself to paint or even draw when he was out. With her mother, sisters, and their families living nearby, however, it was easy to involve herself in their lives. Even then the walls closed in on her, and she found herself wishing for some escape that never came.

A few years earlier, she had started to keep a journal with the hope that writing daily would help her figure things out. Although the process itself had been somewhat rewarding and given her a record of her experiences, it hadn't produced any new insights. It hadn't given her the answers she needed.

Somehow, it seemed, she had lost herself. Worse than that, she didn't know how to find a true sense of herself again. Faint anxiety permeated each day and troubled her dreams at night. It never really left.

The teakettle's whistle roused her from her musings. She crossed the room and grasped the blue and white porcelain handle to remove the kettle from the stove before she switched it off. The cupboard to the left held a multitude of teas, and she selected a packet of mint roibus.

While she busied herself with the tea preparations, she looked thoughtfully at her journal where it lay on the kitchen table. She set her cup beside it and opened to a journal entry from earlier that week.

> August 6, 1996
>
> As I sip the organic orange tea Conner brought back from his research trip last spring, I try to examine my life. It astonishes me how quickly the time has passed. I was a teenager and now a woman. A woman on the brink of a new beginning. Imagine. More schooling at my age! Is there a point in life when it's too late? Can one grow too old in one's own mind and attitudes to accept a challenge or make a change? Am I just lazy with complacency or too paralyzed to accomplish something in life? I imagine myself metaphorically standing beside scholars and artists, and I see myself as a child who stands next to giants. In knowledge, wisdom, understanding, and insight,

> I am but a midget. I feel that the story of my life consists of a phrase I once heard: "I had a small talent that I didn't develop."

She repeated that disturbing final line to herself and then muttered to herself defensively. "I'm doing the best I can. If Conner doesn't support my God-given talents, what am I supposed to do? I'll train in psychology and get a paycheque he can accept."

Anyway, today she would leave with Muffin for an adventure that would give her the opportunity to get herself together. Time in the clear mountain air. Time and space to figure things out. When she got back, things would be better. Her joy would return and she would go to graduate school. Maybe the old adage was true and distance really did make the heart grow fonder. Maybe she and Conner would wonderfully reconnect upon her return.

Another darker thought came to mind, too, but she refused to consider it. She had gotten married to stay married.

She made a quick decision to make fresh waffles for breakfast, her special recipe—a food gift of love to say farewell for the week.

Three

It was almost eight o'clock before Annabel's camping gear, large burgundy suitcase, and cooler rested on the pavement in front of her blue hatchback car. Spatially adept, she was able to fit almost all the items in the small compartment. Only Muffin's traveling carrier had to be relegated to the backseat, and her suitcase sat on the floor on the opposite side. A large water container for the dog and plastic carrying bag with lunch and snacks awaited them on the floor in front of the passenger seat.

Annabel tucked her hands into the back pockets of her jeans, feeling satisfied with her efforts. She looked up as Conner came down the front steps of their white two-story house. His expression was neutral, but she knew he still wasn't comfortable with her solo trip.

He stopped and watched her, noting that she was slim enough to be mistaken for fourteen. Her pretty face was almost in silhouette as she stood with her back to the east. The intense sun caught the gold streaks in her dark blonde hair, creating a halo around her head.

Like a tiny angel, he thought, a lump rising in his throat that made it hard to swallow.

He handed her a small wad of bills. She looked up questioningly as he placed it in her right hand and folded his own elegant hand over it.

"Just-in-case money," he said quietly. "You can buy yourself something or stay at a hotel if things aren't the way you want them to be." He hoped she got his drift.

"Thanks. This is very thoughtful of you."

He drew her into his arms and held her a long moment. Inexplicably, he felt sadder than he should. If anything happened to her, he would never forgive himself for having suggested this stupid trip.

"I should get Muffin from the house and then get going before it gets too hot." Her voice was a mere whisper.

"Yes. That would be wise, Annabel. I'll get her."

He returned a few minutes later leading the small dog on her leash. Muffin galloped down the steps and ran to the boulevard huffing and pulling against the lead. Her full multicoloured coat was nicely brushed and she was ready to go for a car ride.

Annabel picked her up and placed her on the passenger seat. The dog looked questioningly at Conner as if to ask whether he was coming. He leaned down and kissed the back of her silky head.

"Not this time, sweetie."

"We'd better be off," Annabel said somewhat wistfully. "It's at least six hours to Banff from Edmonton."

Conner came around the car and wrapped his wife in a hug. How she wished it could be like this always and not just because she was going away for a few days.

She reminded herself that she had promised that she would try to keep positive. Giving him the best smile she could, she kissed him quickly. Then she detached from him and pushed her long, wavy hair back with both hands.

"I'll call you when I get there, okay?" she said.

"Right."

She climbed into the driver's seat, strapped on the seatbelt, and started the engine.

As she drove slowly down the street, she glanced into the rearview mirror. Conner stood in the middle of the road, his hand caught in a wave midair. She told herself that everything would be okay… and she hoped it was true.

Soon Annabel was on the outskirts of the city, heading south toward Red Deer. As her car ate up the kilometres, she recalled the episode of learning to set up the tent the previous morning. They had gone out into the backyard with Conner carrying the cardboard box that contained the tent to the middle of the lawn. A robin sang in the lilac bush on the north side of the property and the fragrance of annuals in the flowerbeds filled the air, not to mention the hanging pot full of freesia and violet and pink petunias.

She smiled to recall the yard, especially the little porch that was three steps up from the sidewalk. A clothesline was strung across the yard to the lopsided single garage; the structure was built on a wood foundation that had begun to sink. Annabel had looked up, wondering whether that clothesline would get in the way.

Conner had unrolled the dome tent onto the dew-laden grass.

"Let me do it," she said.

"You have to lay it out straight first."

"Okay, I got it."

But Conner couldn't seem to let her do it by herself. He became impatient with her blunders and stood with his arms crossed over his chest and a stiff grimace. She kept repeating to him that she wouldn't learn if she didn't do it herself.

Finally, he sat on the grass and wrapped his arms around his bent knees and watched her. She inserted the three poles, one by one, and then tried to heave the tent up. That was when the top of the dome got stuck on a wire that poked out from the clothesline, snagging the tent.

Conner rose up from the damp grass and gave a snort. "This is not going to work!" he said, trying to control his voice.

God, give me patience, he prayed silently.

"It won't unless you let me try it myself," she replied.

"If you rip the top of the tent, it won't be weatherproof anymore. I don't want to buy a new tent."

"Okay, okay. Calm down. I'll move the whole thing over a few feet and start again."

She heaved the pile of nylon and metal poles over and restarted. Conner sat on the sidelines, his face showing signs of irritation—but he kept his hands out of it, with great effort.

When she finally had the tent erected, with everything done except for the ground pegs, she wanted to let out a whoop of victory. Instead she turned and gave him an I-told-you-so look.

"It's going to be harder up in the mountains all by yourself," he predicted darkly.

She ignored the comment and instead entered the tent. She imagined how great it was going to be to sleep in this large domed tent with her beloved Muffin. The roof was high enough to walk around. She turned slowly, head back and arms outstretched. The zipper could be undone to open the dome to the night sky. Nighttime stargazing was a definite possibility. It certainly beat the fluorescent glow of stars people pasted on their bedroom ceilings these days. She allowed herself to delight in this momentary optimism and again promised herself to be more positive.

Behind the wheel, Annabel roused herself from her musings and stared off at the grey stretch of highway in front of her. She rolled her shoulders a few times and smiled at her companion, asleep on the passenger seat.

"Lord God," she prayed softly, "please keep us safe. Let me learn what I need to learn on this trip."

A sign for Red Deer appeared on the right side of the road, affirming that she was making good time.

Annabel passed the turnoff for Sylvan Lake and knew this meant she was almost at Gasoline Alley, a well-known stop for travellers. There were restaurants and gas stations on both sides of the highway here and she decided to make a quick stop to fill the tank. As the station came into view, she pushed up on the signal light and slowed before entering the slip road that paralleled the highway.

After fuelling up, Annabel pulled into the shade on the west side of the station. She attached the new leather leash to Muffin's collar, lowered her onto the asphalt, and locked the car doors. There was a manmade hill of dirt and small rocks to the north and Muffin stopped there to relieve herself. She looked back at Annabel before launching into the challenge of the climb.

"So you want to climb a mountain?" Annabel laughed as she followed the little dog up the slope, hoping it wouldn't give way and tumble down on them.

Muffin stopped when she reached the summit. Her tongue hung out of the side of her mouth as she turned to face her owner. She stood on her hindlegs with her front paws pumping up and down.

Annabel picked her up and twirled around. "You are the queen of this mountain and the queen of my heart!"

Muffin replied with a series of *arfs* that made Annabel laugh.

"We had better get you some water after this big climb."

She picked up the dog and carefully descended the dirt pile, realizing that it was higher than it had looked. A cascade of rocks broke loose as her shoes struck against the dirt. It was a relief to reach the bottom safely and enter the shade where she had parked the car.

After filling the portable water dish and letting Muffin finish it, she grabbed a bottle of water from the cooler in the hatch. She squinted up at the sun and drained half of the bottle. Although still early, the day was growing warm. It was time to go.

She stowed the empty water bottle in the hatch before she closed it. They were on their way in minutes.

Annabel turned the air conditioner on low before she joined the highway at the end of the ramp and picked up speed. She continued south toward Calgary, mindful that there was still a long way to go before they reached their destination.

Her thoughts drifted again. Long-distance driving had a way of opening the mind and all sorts of memories rose to the surface unbidden—the kind of memories one rarely revisits.

Annabel had shown signs of artistic talent even at the tender age of six. She remembered the day she had walked home with her first-grade teacher, Mrs. Jordan, who had lived on the same block as Annabel's family. It had been a thrill! Mrs. Jordan had asked her about her latest art project, an ink drawing of pussy willows. What had been her inspiration? Annabel knew the answer.

"We go to my baba's farm and on the way back my daddy always cuts pussy willows from the ditch for my mommy. She loves them and they make us think about my baba."

"I see," said Mrs. Jordan, "And is your baba your grandmother."

"Yes, she is. It's Ukrainian." Annabel spoke the word carefully. "She lives on a farm far away from here, near St. Paul."

"Do you get to visit her very often?"

"As much as we can. Sometimes she comes to our house, too. When we go there, we get to see all the farm animals."

"How exciting! And of course, those lovely pussy willows."

Annabel giggled and nodded her head.

The following week, Mrs. Jordan had stopped in front of their house to chat while Annabel helped her mother pick weeds from a flowerbed. The young teacher commented to her mother how mature Annabel's drawing of pussy willows was for such a young child. Her mother had smiled and agreed that her daughter certainly was creative.

As a teenager, art had become Annabel's favourite pastime, and eventually her identity. In high school, she'd stayed in the art classroom even through lunch breaks to work on independent projects. Her one goal had been to be an artist.

All by herself, she had investigated postsecondary art programs and found the Alberta College of Art and Design, an elite school in Calgary. In her final year of high school, she'd ordered their hands-on entrance exam, passed with flying colours, and gained acceptance for the coming year.

Annabel had been fully convinced that this was God's plan for her.

As graduation drew near, she met a boy who fell head over heels for her. Scott hadn't been a Christian, but he was fun and athletic. He'd been scouted by professional football teams and seemed to have a promising future—and he wanted to marry her right after graduation. She had laughed at that and assured him she was too young to marry, but it had been an exciting summer of laughter and youthful passion.

Annabel had known she didn't really love him, but she'd ended up confused and ignored that confusion. Life with a professional athlete had seemed glamorous.

It had been a mistake not to seek advice from anyone. Spending no time in prayer about it had been an even bigger one.

She withdrew from art school before the first term began in autumn. Then Scott received notice that he was being drafted onto a team in Eastern Canada. Their ill-fated romance then ended abruptly with apologies and weak promises of a long-distance relationship.

With mixed feelings, Annabel had given up on her life with Scott—and in her heart, she knew that God had stopped her from marrying the wrong person. She wasn't to be unequally yoked with an unbeliever, no matter how handsome and exciting he was.

Her future was now uncertain. With deep remorse, she realized that she had given up on her own dreams, and that became the greater pain. She had squandered her coveted place in art school. It was over. A sense of hopelessness covered her soul like a gossamer veil.

Annabel never found the courage to pursue entrance to art college again. After a few years of working office jobs, she attended a local community college where she earned a diploma in graphic design. She justified the decision as being practical. It gave her an opportunity to build a career.

But that had never been satisfying. Design jobs were scarce, and it seemed like the best ones went to graduates from the art college in Calgary.

After years of low-paying positions and making no career progress, she began to earn additional credits to upgrade to a bachelor of arts degree, taking one course at a time. Her enthusiasm was lacklustre, though. Her potential for art had gone untapped. Fine art remained just a dream, and one she reached for no longer.

"I haven't thought about these things in forever," Annabel muttered as the car barrelled down the highway. "Too much thinking isn't good for a person."

A few minutes later, a sign appeared showing the remaining distance to Calgary.

Talk about timing, Lord.

Her thoughts faded away and the uneasy, despondent feeling that had increasingly permeated her life reemerged. Somehow along the way she had lost a sense of her artistic identity. She sometimes felt as though she needed to reinvent herself. In fact, she had written a poem in her journal recently that expressed it all. She recited some of the words:

"Imagination entangled with reality,
a new image unfolds
a new creation born
of life's weary struggles
a new self."

Was that what she was trying to do, reinvent herself? Is that why she was headed for a master's degree in psychology?

"I should be so thankful," she mused aloud. "I'm one of a handful of students chosen for a very competitive program."

She sighed and loosened her grip on the steering wheel.

One month after applying for the counselling program, she had received the call for an interview. She and two other prospective students fielded an hour of questions from two of the program's professors. It had been a rough ride. None of the candidates had known how many of them would be admitted, leaving Annabel to feel terrified of her chances.

Thanks to her mother's prayers, she came through successfully as one of the top three candidates. And it all lay in front of her one month hence.

Yet she still wondered why she had even applied for it.

Realizing she had tightened her grip on the steering wheel again, Annabel pressed her teeth firmly together, her lips turning in a frown. She grimly pulled herself together as she remembered her promise to be more positive. She could interpret all these memories as a kind of spiritual therapy. That would fit with her new future.

She would arrive in Calgary, the place of her lost dreams, in half an hour. She cast her eyes to the left at rolling fields. The words *wheat* and *chaff* briefly caressed her mind. A bright streak of yellow across the middle distance made the crops look as though the sunlight's touch was bringing them to life.

"What a painting that would make! The brilliant golds and sombre ochres. The dark greens of the surrounding foliage. The yellow greens near the ditch. And that absolutely brilliant stroke of yellow on the field. An azure sky…"

The sound of her voice filled the quietness of the car. She surprised herself. The description seemed to awaken her artistic sensibilities. She knew she was touching something deep inside, something that had been hidden for a long time. A slow smile tipped up the corners of her mouth and spread across her face. She shook her head, making her long curls bounce. It paid to be positive. This trip might be exactly what she needed.

Four

The Rocky Mountains stood boldly before her in all their majesty. The scene had a poignant beauty. The sun tinged the snow-caps with a pale pink that stood in stark contrast to the resonant greens and greys.

Annabel turned right off the Trans-Canada Highway and then took a left before the overpass. A short distance further, she slowed down for the Texas gate, a gap in the road covered by a series of metal rods meant to control wildlife. Ahead, the road curved into the town of Banff. It was a familiar and welcoming sight.

"I had better secure a tenting site up at Tunnel Mountain before I do anything else," she muttered as she rotated her shoulders back to ease the stiffness that resulted from sitting in one spot for hours.

Almost six hours in all. Annabel had driven straight through from Red Deer with no further stops. And Muffin had slept the whole way.

The sun beat down from a cloudless cerulean blue sky, her favourite paint colour. At home she had tubes of it in every paint medium—watercolour, oil, and acrylics.

It had been worth the long drive to get here early in the day. Perhaps later she would even take on the challenge of creating some art. Maybe "later" would actually happen this time.

She turned left off Banff Avenue, the main road, before the temptation of the shopping district could lay hold of her. She followed the curve of the road up the mountain to the point where it levelled off and housed various types of accommodations and restaurants. Afterward there was nothing but nature and a deep valley whose beauty captured her artistic eye.

Annabel knew she had to keep watch for the sign for the National Park campground so she wouldn't miss it. She glanced at her watch. At almost two o'clock, it was already steaming hot. She turned the air conditioner up a notch. It was still pretty close to checkout time as far as she knew, so she thought she would be okay. There would be campsites available.

A large parking lot stretched out beside the road, and beyond it was a broad lookout point with a view of the mountains and valley. She and Conner had watched the fall of meteorites at this very spot several years back. They had cuddled in the small blue car with their dog snoring in her carrier on the back seat. Both of them had expressed how small they felt against the vastness of the sky and the workings of the heavens.

So many memories in this place.

She signalled to turn left into the Tunnel Mountain National Park Campground. There was no lineup of vehicles. That could be a good or a bad sign.

In a few minutes, she pulled up to the window of the small wooden building where a woman in a dull green uniform sat. The glass window slid open.

"I'd like a campsite, please," Annabel said.

"Tent? What section did you want to camp in?"

"I beg your pardon?"

"Family. Young people. Firepits. No firepits. Did you have a preference?

"I'd like one closest to the entrance, please."

"Okay. That's where we generally put the young people."

"No problem. Could I have a site as close to the entrance as possible?"

"Certainly. How many nights?"

"Um, let's say three nights to start."

"That's fine, but make sure you let us know early if you want more nights. It's really busy here in the summer months. And that puts you pretty close to midweek. Many tourists stay a full week." The park attendant's voice took on an official tone. "That's fifteen dollars per night. It comes to forty-seven dollars and twenty-five cents, please."

The park attendant handed her a map and a pamphlet along with her change from a fifty. She leaned forward a bit and pointed toward the paved road ahead.

"First right and your site's straight ahead at the entrance on the inner circle. There are nightly shows in the amphitheatre. Have a look at the schedule to see the subjects and presenters. Oh, and please make sure not to leave any food out at night. We want to keep campers safe from bear visits. Have a pleasant stay."

The woman closed the glass window and turned away to busy herself with paperwork.

Annabel looked at the change in her palm. There was a toonie, a new coin that had replaced the two-dollar bill earlier in the year. She stroked its shiny surface thoughtfully. It was her first one. Perhaps it was a positive sign. She pocketed the coins then proceeded into the park. On her right was a frightening display: a battered food cooler obviously mauled by a bear had been hung above the road with a strongly worded sign to echo the attendant's words.

I must make sure not to leave food exposed at the campsite, she reminded herself.

She suppressed a shudder and instinctively reached out to stroke Muffin, determining to leave food cooler locked in the car. Conner had reminded her that even toothpaste and other toiletries could entice bears. They could smell something like that from up to five miles away, he had said.

She only hoped other campers would be as respectful of the dangers. There were lockup food coolers for hikers, so she supposed everybody would be careful. At least her campsite wasn't on the periphery of the woods, and she hoped it would be well lit.

The site was easy to find, exactly to the left of the entrance on the inner ring of campsites. It was generously sized and had several large cleared spaces suitable for a tent.

Annabel pulled in and then reversed quickly, deciding to back the car in close to the picnic table. She carefully manoeuvred the small vehicle up a slight incline and past a gangly evergreen tree.

"Here at last," she said, stroking Muffin. The little dog, still curled up on the passenger seat, lifted her head with sleepy eyes and thumped her plumed tail. "I'll take you for a little walk. Then I have to set up our tent house, okay?"

She hooked the leash to the dog's brown leather collar, picked her up, and set her on the gravel and dirt path. After she locked the car doors, she pocketed the key.

They headed together along the one-way loop road that led through the sites, taking notice of where everything was situated. It had been a few years since they had camped here. She passed a raised platform with two huge garbage bins with bear-proof handles. There was a tap with a sign that read "Drinking Water" with a drain beneath. The building that housed the washrooms and showers was halfway around the loop. She found campsites on both sides of the road, and most of the sites were already taken. Again, Annabel was thankful she had arrived early in the day.

They arrived back at their site within fifteen minutes. It had been good to stretch her legs and let go of the stress of long-distance driving.

Annabel knew that the best thing to do was to set up the tent right away. That way she could relax and have time to rest a little before heading back into town to look around. She knew that was what Conner would do.

"You stay in the car until I have our abode set up," she said protectively to Muffin. The little dog settled again on the passenger seat after turning around several times. She was such a sweet, obedient little companion.

Annabel lifted the back hatch of the car and began to remove the necessary items. She put the tent box, hammer, and tarp on the wooden picnic table, being careful to avoid the white bird stains on the dark wood, and then returned to shut the hatch. She didn't need any distractions.

The first step was to remove the tent from the box and sort the poles. Frowning with concentration, she lost herself in connecting the folded poles. They were joined by elastic rope and it was a challenge to keep all the parts in the right place at the right time. She tried to remember if it had been this hard at home.

"Lord, please help me. I have to do it by myself this time. No choice now. No Conner to bail me out."

Finally, the pieces came together and she carefully laid out the large nylon tent.

Before she could get any further, though, a slight movement in her peripheral vision caught her attention. She turned her head slightly to the left and saw a man seated on top of the picnic table across the road from her. He threw his head back and took a drink from the can in his hand, then resumed watching her.

She tossed her head with indignation, more determined than before to get the tent up. An audience was certainly not appreciated in the least. It made her feel nervous and even incompetent.

Annabel stood with her hands on her slim hips and surveyed the situation. The ground was a little sloped, and she realized she would need to move the whole tent over. Gripping the sides, she dragged the nylon to the left, trying to ignore the man's impertinence.

The first pole went in easily and the jointed pieces stayed together. The second pole made the tent rise from the ground, and surprisingly the third one stabilized it. Momentarily, Annabel felt akin to Superwoman.

She returned to the table to get a tent peg and glanced again across the road. The man was now standing. He seemed very tall and had thick blond hair that waved back from a strong, handsome face. He was very different from her Conner, whose well-bred manners would never allow him to stare at a stranger. She decided it was best to ignore him even though he was watching her intently.

With the small silver engineering hammer in her right hand, she placed the tent peg through the first loop on the right side of the tent. She raised the hammer and banged the head of the peg. It was thick and made of bright yellow plastic. The peg sank into the surface of the ground only a few inches. She swung the hammer again, but it wouldn't go in farther. She felt impatient embarrassment arise but tried to stifle it.

She walked back to the table and picked up three more large yellow pegs. She placed one in the next loop and tried to bang it into the ground with the little hammer. Again, it barely stayed erect and refused to enter the rocky soil.

Annabel worked her way around the tent. She managed to get one of the pegs to penetrate the soil, but the rest were impossible to set in place. She felt perspiration bead on her forehead. Her hands were a little shaky.

"As if I needed that guy over there watching me," she muttered darkly.

Frustration began to work its way through her. She walked back to her starting point, crouched down, and swung the hammer high to bang it hard onto the peg again and again. The soil was replete with rocks. How in the world was she going to get these pegs in? This was a mountain, for goodness sake. It was just as Conner had warned.

Suddenly, a shadow crossed over her. She paused, her hand with the hammer poised in the air.

"Okay. I tried to stay out of it, and I usually would, but you do seem to be in trouble here."

Annabel lowered her arm and twisted her crouched body around as she gazed up. It was the man from the picnic table. She couldn't quite place his soft European accent.

Oh great, she thought sarcastically. *Just what I need—the audience to crowd in on me!*

"I beg your pardon?" she said.

"I usually just stay to myself when I'm not working. I'm an adventure travel guide, you see. But I've been watching your struggle with the tent pegs." He kicked his leather boot at one of the yellow pegs. "It's the wrong kind. You need the large metal ones for camping in the mountains."

He ran his left hand through his thick, wavy hair. He had the most brilliant blue eyes Annabel had ever seen.

She smiled and rose to her feet. "Well, they're the only pegs I have."

"They won't do. You'll have to go to town and buy proper ones. Give me the hammer. I'll do it for you."

"Honestly, I'm fine…"

He interrupted by stepping forward and taking hold of the silver hammer. His biceps bulged from under his white T-shirt as he flexed his right arm. With a forceful swing, he beat the peg into the ground. He then stepped to the right and attacked the next one. Unfortunately, the plastic broke under the strength of the blow. He looked up at her with his piercing blue eyes, no trace of remorse evident.

"I told you. Wrong pegs." He worked his way around the tent, breaking several more pegs in the process. "You have to put the tarp up next."

"Yes, I realize that," she replied, trying not to sound sharp.

She walked slowly to the table to get the bundled tarp, and then returned to where he waited. She stood before him like a miniature doll, the pile of plastic tarp a barrier between them. He reached out to take it from her. She released it and pushed her hair back from her face.

"You're not as young as I thought at first," he said in a matter-of-fact tone. "But still very attractive."

She couldn't believe what she was hearing. Caught off-guard, it took her a few moments to pull her dignity together. What nerve he had.

"I beg your pardon?"

"You are not as young as you looked from over there," he said more slowly as he motioned with his left arm toward his picnic table. "But you are still very attractive. It's a compliment."

"Oh, a compliment. I see. Thanks."

Annabel didn't know what else to say. She wasn't that old; she wasn't even forty. But suddenly she felt embarrassed. He stood looking down at her, and the silence felt uncomfortable.

"Well, you have beautiful blue eyes," she blurted out.

She froze. What in the world had made her say such a forward thing to a perfect stranger? And she was a married woman. She had noticed his intense eyes, but she hadn't meant to say anything about them out loud. It was an awkward moment following an impulsive gesture.

He smiled before he threw the tarp over the side of the tent. Looking over his shoulder at her, his mouth curled up higher on one side.

"Thank you. That's a very nice thing to say."

Annabel put her hands into her back pockets and looked down at the ground. She shrugged her shoulders and then walked around the tent to help secure the tarp with thin metal pins that easily penetrated the rocky soil. She couldn't decide if he was a good angel sent to help her or just an unwanted interruption. She decided to swallow her impulsive words, her pride, and be thankful either way.

They were done in short order, and she realized they hadn't even introduced themselves. She looked up into his eyes and allowed herself to smile.

"I'm Annabel," she said, extending her right hand.

He looked at her tiny hand stretching toward him and smiled broadly. Then he reached his arm toward her. "I'm Jan."

They shook hands. His large hand, calloused on the palm, enclosed her smooth small one.

Annabel took a step back instinctively. "So is that some sort of European accent I detect?"

"Yes. I'm from the Netherlands."

It was a curious word. Netherlands. She mulled it over. It sounded like netherworld, the place where bad spirits dwelled. Or where unlawful activity happened. Annabel felt a slight caution in her heart. Was he just a human being or could he be from the dark side? She felt a fleeting panic before she realized she was just being silly. He could be good news or bad news. It really wasn't her business.

Jan interrupted her musing by clearing his throat and Annabel realized she had been staring at him, her eyes wide. What would he think of her now? Old and senile?

"Netherlands. Holland," he said. "I come from close to Amsterdam. You know. Tulips and windmills. Wooden shoes. That sort of thing."

He was playing with her, and she disliked being the target of his joke. It made her feel provincial, even backward. She had done a bit of traveling before she got married.

"Yes, of course. I've been there twice. We spent a week in Amsterdam, visiting the Van Gogh museum and Rembrandt's house, among other things."

His blonde eyebrows rose and then lowered. "A world traveller then?"

He was getting to her. Since her blundering comment about his eyes, she had felt self-conscious and somewhat defensive.

She nodded her head. "Yup. I guess so. Well, thanks so much, Jan, for helping out a damsel in distress."

"Damsel in distress. So you believe in fairy stories?"

"Not really, but just … well, thanks for helping me out."

She was annoyed that he had broken the tent pegs, but there was nothing to do now but replace them. His help had come with a cost.

"No problem."

"Well, I'd better get into town to buy tent pegs." She motioned with her right hand toward her car.

"Invest a little money and get the right kind. They need to be heavy metal, the kind that go in at an angle. There is a camping supply store on the main street. They can help you pick out the right ones."

"Okay. Thanks again."

He stood still and continued to look intently into her eyes. Before embarrassment could bloom on her cheeks as a blush, she waved quickly and walked toward her car. Immediately, she put the key into the ignition.

Is he going to stay at my campsite all day? she wondered.

"I can go with you," he called. "If you want?"

She rolled down the window. "Thank you, but I'll be fine. I'm certain you have better things to do than spend your time in a camping store looking at tent pegs."

He shrugged and turned away.

She looked over to his site as he crossed the road. There was a large pile of beer cans under one tree. Some were empties, but more than half were still full. She had a good idea what Jan would be doing that afternoon.

Annabel started her car and inched it forward down the slope, around the corner, and out of the campsite. She felt relieved to be out of there.

FIVE

The sidewalks were crowded with tourists. Many of them wore the latest coloured sunglasses which made their faces look like a moving rainbow. Vehicles lined the streets and filled the parking lot near the bridge. Annabel drove up and down until she found a spot on a side street near the river a few blocks off Banff Avenue. It was well shaded and cool so Muffin would be okay with the windows rolled down a bit, at least for a brief time.

As she walked the short distance to the camping store, her eyes took in the sights. There were restaurants and shops of all kinds, and the smell of fresh baked goods from a coffee place reminded her that she hadn't had lunch. But it was the towering mountains that surrounded and dwarfed the little town that most inspired her. Her family had been coming here since she was a little girl, but the mountains never lost their appeal.

Annabel paused a moment and looked north toward Mount Norquay. It had once been her dream to climb a mountain right to the top, to experience that sense of conquest. It was an existential idea: woman against nature. She laughed softly and quoted aloud from the book of Psalms: *"I will raise my eyes to the mountains; from where will my help come? My help comes from the Lord, who made heaven and earth."*[1] The mountains were certainly beautiful, even if she never climbed one. Did they hold the answers she needed?

As she passed an art gallery, Annabel felt a stirring in her heart. She gave it a wistful glance and remembered driving past the art

---

[1] Psalm 121:1–2.

college in Calgary that very morning. If she could just find the artist inside her again, maybe everything in life would change.

Graduate school is the mountain I have to climb, she whispered to the soaring heights. *Art is the one I want to climb.*

A crow flew upward from a nearby tree, an ebony streak against the clear sky. It gave a raucous call as though in agreement. Being an artist again seemed as impossible as climbing one of these majestic mountains. Just more unfulfilled dreams.

Annabel sighed deeply as she considered ascending a real mountain. She didn't even know if there were trails that led to the top of these rocky structures. But the idea did appeal to her. The mountains seemed to call her into their mysterious embrace. She had undertaken hikes of various lengths, but never a climb. Would the adventures of this trip include one? It didn't seem likely. It would be a miracle if she could even pull out a pencil and create a sketch. That was something she could aim for. It was actually possible.

The young man at the camping store easily picked out suitable tent pegs after having a good laugh at her debacle. He even demonstrated how to hold the hammer and strike a blow that would keep the tent secure.

After pleasant conversation about travel and camping, she returned to her car. Muffin was awake now and whining. It was definitely time for a walk.

Annabel put her Bible under her left arm and took the leash in her right hand. Together, she and her beloved companion set out along the sidewalk that followed the curve of the Bow River northward. She found a wooden bench in exactly the right place beneath the dense shade of two mighty evergreens. It wasn't a difficult decision to sit a while there and rest.

She put the little dog on the bench and sat beside her before opening her Bible and reading from Isaiah 6.

> Holy, Holy, Holy, is the Lord of armies. The whole earth is full of His glory.[2]

She gazed around at the myriad trees, bushes, wildflowers, and mountains. In the quietude, she listened to the joy-filled song of the river as it rushed by then caught itself in the cluster of rocks, whispering its tune.

Her heart agreed with the prophet's words. Nature certainly showed forth God's glory. Her eyes grew moist and tears fell onto her smooth cheeks. She wiped them away with the back of her hand and then flipped to the Psalms, her favourite book. She read quietly the words in Psalm 37:

> Delight yourself in the Lord; and He will give you the desires of your heart. Commit your way to the Lord, trust also in Him, and He will do it.[3]

"What do I want?" She breathed out the words, but there was no reply. A slight breeze rustled the branches and caused her to look up as the leaves performed a momentary lazy dance. "Lord, do You know what I want? What is the true desire of my heart? What do I need?"

She heard no reply from heaven. What she knew was that she was going to be a graduate student next month regardless of how she felt. Despite the dread and anxiety that sometimes squeezed her heart, it was the decided path. Art would blend into the background of life once more.

The shadows were beginning to lengthen when she raised her delicate arms and stretched. Annabel glanced at her watch. It was past six o'clock.

---

[2] Isaiah 6:5.

[3] Psalm 37:4–5.

"Well, my little Muffin. Do you want to get some dinner?"

A whimper and pleading brown eyes followed the question. The little dog climbed onto her lap and lifted her head to reach Annabel's cheeks where the salty tears had left a residue. Gently, she licked it away.

Annabel hugged Muffin before she put her onto the grass. "Right. Then let's get back to our campsite."

There was no argument. The tiny dog pulled away from the bench, ready to retrace their steps along the scenic pathway back to the car.

Annabel breathed in the fresh mountain air and for the first time in a very long while felt the beginnings of relaxation deep within her. She blew out a long stream of air. The flowing river drew her again into its melodic song, the harsh bark of a crow commanded attention, and the deepening greens of the forest spoke untold mysteries. The sun continued shining in its full intensity despite the harkening call of dusk. The scene was a feast for the eyes and the heart.

At this moment, Annabel was glad she had come away to this mountain town. She felt at one with this enticing environment, where her memories extended all the way back to childhood. Here was history and here was the potential for renewal. A portal to a better future.

After she opened the car door and let her dog scamper onto the passenger seat, Annabel closed her eyes and repeated the psalmist's words in a silent prayer.

"I will delight myself in the Lord, and He will give me the desires of my heart. Lord, show me my true desire. I've wasted so much time and have arrived nowhere in life. Help me to find the way."

She breathed deeply as she proceeded down the road slowly. She didn't really know where this little vacation would take her. It was tentative, but she was beginning to feel alive again.

SIX

It was well into early evening when they reached the campsite. Annabel sat in the car a few minutes thinking about what she would have for dinner. First, she would warm up Muffin's food with hot water from the kettle to make gravy for it. Just the way the dog liked it.

Considering the long drive, the challenges of the tent, and the time, she quickly decided to have vegetarian cup of soup with a cheese bagel loaded with lettuce, tomato, and cucumber slices. She had made it for lunch in the morning but hadn't eaten it.

Still preoccupied with her culinary thoughts, Annabel opened the car door. As she climbed out, she stepped onto the toes of worn leather hiking boots instead of dirt and rocks.

"What in the world?" she muttered with a hint of irritation. It quickly mingled with embarrassment when she looked up to spot Jan from the Netherlands. Why hadn't she been paying attention?

"I've been waiting for you," he said with a twinkle in his intense blue eyes.

"Waiting for me?" she blurted out. "Why would you do that?" Confusion covered the words and blurred them together in her mind.

"To help you with your tent pegs."

She pushed her hair back off her face with both hands and stepped sideways to shift her stance on the rocky ground away from him.

"Oh, I'll be fine. The man at the camping store gave me all the information I need."

"But not the muscle to put the right pegs into this impenetrable ground."

Jan flexed his right arm and grinned. Emotionally, it threw her off-balance, but she quickly composed herself. She wasn't going to let him befuddle her.

"He showed me how to hold the hammer to get the pegs in correctly, too."

"I insist on helping a damsel in distress."

She shook her head a few times in defeat, regretting her use of the metaphor earlier that day. "Okay then, how can I refuse?"

Annabel wanted to refuse. Something in her spirit warned her that the few letters in this man's name could spell trouble. But common politeness begged her to accept his offer.

It took him just a few minutes to bang the pegs past the resistance of the rocky soil. He then threw the spoiled plastic pegs onto the picnic table and they landed with a clatter. Afterward he looked at her thoughtfully, swinging his hammer. She watched him, knowing by the look in his eyes that he was attracted to her.

A smile spread over his generous mouth. There was no doubt that she would look attractive with the evening sun behind her, lighting her fair hair and transforming her slim figure into an elegant silhouette.

Just thank him and get on with making dinner, she scolded herself. She felt defenceless standing there, the silence creating a gap between them that begged to be filled.

"Thanks for your help," she said. "I'm sorry that you felt you needed to interrupt your vacation time."

"You're welcome. Have you already eaten?"

Annabel's head jerked back in surprise. She hadn't been expecting the change in topic.

"I was just about to attend to that matter," she replied forcing herself to smile.

Inwardly she chastised herself for not telling him she had eaten in town. It wasn't the truth, but it wasn't his business either.

"I wanted to invite the damsel to dinner." His smile showed that he was pleased with himself.

"Oh, I couldn't do that." She paused, then raised her left hand and wiggled her fingers. "Husband. Married."

"Husband?" He glanced down at her left hand and took in the golden band on her ring finger. "Do you mean some rich, fat businessman who lets his wife confront the dangers of the wilderness by herself?"

Of all the nerve. Annabel instantly felt protective of her handsome husband and defensive of their marriage. She took a step back and folded her arms over her chest. A frown marred the beauty of her features.

"I didn't mean to offend," he said. "It's just that I often meet women with such husbands in my line of work. It's a simple invitation to dinner from one camper to another."

When she didn't answer, he glanced over at the phone booth located beside the washroom facilities building.

"Why don't you call and ask him for permission to accept the humble offer?"

She hesitated. She hadn't come away to spend time with a stranger, even a nice-looking one with beautiful blue eyes. She was a happily married woman, after all, wasn't she? A good Christian wife.

But this could be her way out. Conner wouldn't easily agree to her spending time with a strange man.

"Are you afraid of me?" he taunted.

She lifted her chin in mock defiance. "Of course not. Should I be?"

"You never know." He grinned as he continued to swing the hammer. "Why don't you call him and ask permission, if that's what you're expected to do?"

Annabel felt indecisive and foolish. Conner had been correct. She was fragile, perhaps too much so to have come away by herself. She hadn't anticipated Jan from the Netherlands.

Jan moved side to side, his leather boots crunching on the small stones as he waited for her reply. It had now become something akin to a dare. Conner was her safety net. Annabel was certain that he would tell her to stay at her own campsite. He would get her out of this increasingly tense situation.

"Well, I think that's exactly what I'll do."

She unrolled the window a bit, then slammed and locked the car door. With a determined stride, she made her way to the payphone. As she entered the small booth, she looked back toward her car, hoping that Muffin was okay with the slight delay of dinner.

Why couldn't she just have given a firm refusal?

She heard the telephone ringing and wondered if Conner would be home.

"Hello," he finally answered.

"Will you accept a collect call from …" The automated question was followed by her own soft voice reciting her name. "… Annabel."

"Yes."

"Conner, it's me. I made it here okay."

"Good. Is everything all right? You're calling late. How is Muffin?"

"Fine and waiting for her dinner."

"Tent up?"

She detected a note of scepticism in his voice. "Actually, yes, it is."

"Oh. So you managed okay by yourself then?"

"Well, mostly. Those plastic tent pegs broke in the rocky ground."

"Then how are you keeping the tent from blowing away?"

Annabel could feel the edges of irritation beginning to hem her in. She needed him to be her hero, and he wanted her to fail. She fought to keep her voice positive and light.

"I was rescued by another camper who suggested that metal pegs are a better choice for mountain camping. So I drove to town and got some. I hope that's okay."

He didn't reply, so she continued on.

"It's this tour guide from the Netherlands. Now he's suggesting that I join him at his campsite for dinner. What an idea." She forced herself to laugh.

"If you want to visit with another camper, go ahead. I trust you, sunshine."

Annabel hadn't expected that at all. "Are you sure?"

"Yes, it would be good to have a bit of company. You've been to the Netherlands. Maybe you could talk about Vincent Van Gogh."

"Um, okay, I guess. I'll make it a short visit and then get to bed early."

"Remember to dress warm enough. It will grow cooler in the evening. Have a good night and call me tomorrow."

"I'll do that."

"I love you, Annabel."

She paused a moment. "Me too, Conner. Good night."

"Good night."

As she hung up the receiver, she wondered if she ought to have told Conner more about this stranger.

Like what? she asked herself. *That he's handsome, strong, and tall with beautiful blue eyes and thick gorgeous hair?*

She could still get herself out of it by lying. She could say her husband had said no. But it wasn't really a date or anything. It was just food at a picnic table.

Her mother would say that she was starting to rationalize. It was a sign that she was heading down the wrong path. She mulled it over, but weariness was beating down her resolve. She didn't like the stress she was feeling over it.

It's just dinner, and it saves me having to do it myself, she told herself, forgetting that, except for adding water to her soup, her dinner was ready.

Jan was waiting beside the table on her site, drumming his fingers on the worn, stained wood.

He looked up as she approached. "Well?"

She paused and sighed with a bit of a huff. "Okay, but I need to feed my dog first."

"I'll get started cooking then. Come over when you're ready." He motioned with his head in the direction of his site. "See you later."

Annabel opened the hatch of her car and rummaged through the food box to find a can of dog food, the can opener, and the kettle. She stuck the opener into the back pocket of her jeans, then poured water from the large container into the kettle. Holding the can and kettle in her left hand, she picked up Muffin and secured her under her right arm.

"Come on, my girl. Let's get you some dinner," she said in a perky voice as they headed through the trees to the washroom building to boil the water. Then she muttered, "How in the world did I get us into this situation?"

It didn't take long to feed her dog. She sat on the picnic bench for a while, afterwards she gave Muffin treats one by one. How she wished Conner had saved her from the evening ahead. Although she really just wanted to be alone, she didn't know how to back out gracefully. The evening ahead was set.

SEVEN

What does a married woman wear to eat dinner with a stranger in the woods at the top of a mountain? A married Christian woman? Annabel decided to add a thick hand-knitted sweater over her T-shirt and jeans. Its muted tones blended with the expanding dusk. The air was growing cooler, as Conner had reminded her.

Holding her dog in her arms with the leash wrapped around her right wrist, she made her way across the gravel road. Jan was hunched over a pot at the grill, but he turned to her as soon as her foot crossed the boundary into his camp.

"Why did you bring the dog?"

The blunt question made her want to turn on her heels and leave immediately. Instead she stopped and stared directly at him, her eyes flashing.

"I beg your pardon? I came camping with her. I'm certainly not going to leave her alone!"

"All right. I guess I'm stuck with a dog for the evening."

"We can both leave, if that's what you prefer."

"No, I'll live with it."

He was annoyed, but Annabel didn't care. Maybe this was the sign she needed to regain her senses, return to her own campsite, and just go to bed without supper. In fact, that was a great idea. She was about to turn and leave when he spoke again.

"Have a seat."

He gestured toward the picnic table. It was set with a plain blue cloth, blue ironware camping plates, transparent plastic cups, and metal cutlery.

"Do you want wine or beer?" he asked.

"Neither, thanks. I'll just have water, if you have some."

He grunted. "There's all kinds of pop over by the tree."

And all kinds of beer, she told herself.

Annabel rose, walked over to the pile of pop cans, and chose sugar-free ginger ale. As she moved back toward the table, she crossed over the length of his shadow on the rocky soil and rough grass. An uneasy feeling arose in the region of her heart.

Just leave. Flee. Get away from this man now.

The voice was so clear that she looked around to see who had spoken.

Jan had turned back to tend to the food he was cooking. She shook her head and sat on the seat attached to the table. She would look and feel silly running away like a schoolgirl. She would have a bite to eat and then make excuses to leave early.

When she reached for the pop can, Jan cracked open another beer and chugged it down without a pause. An empty silence followed. Annabel stroked her dog's head and leaned down to nuzzle Muffin's face in the long, soft hair. The dog was her tether to reality.

"So what is a beautiful woman doing alone on a mountain camping?"

Annabel wasn't certain what to say. She thought a moment before replying. "Oh, I love to be in the mountains. My husband couldn't get away. So here I am." She gave a weak smile. Her eyebrows rose and caused wrinkles in her forehead.

"Foolish man to let his wife go alone where there are so many unpredictable strangers."

Instantly, Annabel wished she had asked to be in the family section of the campground instead of near the entrance. This part of the park was popular with young people. Not that she was old—she was still in her thirties—but families sounded safer at this moment.

"He's anything but foolish," she said.

Jan let out a long husky laugh as he continued stirring the pot. "We'll see. You already know that I'm a tour guide. What do you do?"

Annabel still felt insecure about telling people she was headed for graduate school to study psychology. He didn't need to know about her inner turmoil over the future. Instead she pulled on her past.

"I'm an artist."

"What kind of artist?"

"A good one." She sniggered.

"I mean, what kind of art?"

"I paint people… mostly."

"People?"

"Figures. Draped and undraped." She paused, then added facetiously, "Do you want to pose for me?"

He stood from his crouching position and turned his full body toward her, making intense eye contact.

She didn't know what she had hoped to gain with that silly, offhand remark. She was the foolish one. Why had she said such a stupid thing? What would Conner say? Gosh, what would God think of her?

Coming for dinner had been a bad idea. A really bad idea.

"No," he replied as he returned to his cooking. "Not me."

Relief flooded her soul. She knew the Lord had saved her from her rash words and imprudent blunder. She wouldn't talk about being an artist anymore. It was too sore a wound to be safe ground for conversation.

While she was lost in her remorse, Jan took the plates from the table. Now he was scraping something onto them that looked remotely like stew. He placed them steaming hot on the table. He shook multigrain buns onto another blue plate.

"Okay, let's eat."

Annabel turned to glance at her car and tent. The desire to run returned, but she faced the table instead. The night air had cooled significantly, so she put Muffin under the bulky sweater. The unattractive shape looked remarkably like she was ready to give birth.

Jan looked down at the bulge with disgust. The evening shadows carved his features into an austere expression. He looked like an ancient marble statue.

He shook his head and sat down. "I'm weary of the people I meet in these places. I usually keep to myself."

Annabel listened but didn't look up. She concentrated on pushing her fork through the food on her plate before tasting it. It was grey-brown and unappealing. Yet the first bite was surprisingly tasty.

"People want to use me all the time," he added. "So I do the same."

Annabel looked up at him. This wasn't typical dinner conversation. Where was this going to lead?

"What exactly do you mean?" she asked cautiously.

"Everywhere I go, someone wants something from me—my time, my attention, anything they can get. Especially the ladies. On my own time, I make sure my needs are met. I use women. Married women. It's what they want. They don't love their husbands anyway. Back in the Netherlands, I do it all the time."

"If you're saying what I think you are, that's terrible! And I never asked you for anything at all!" Her exclamation punctuated the air.

The hot flames in the grill crackled and dissolved her words into the deepening darkness. What was she doing here with this strange man? Instinctively, she placed her hands on her dog, who had fallen asleep beneath her sweater.

"Don't be so naïve," he said. "It's not terrible at all. Look, you're very attractive, even beautiful. Why did you come to dine with me?"

"You asked me. I thought you were just being polite."

"Polite?" His laugh was a snort.

Annabel turned and got up to leave. This whole situation spelled trouble.

"Don't leave," he said.

She turned and glared at him. "What do you expect me to do?"

"Just enjoy the meal. I'm a good cook."

Against her better judgment, she sat back down.

"Eat."

They ate in silence the next five minutes, their metal forks scraped against the blue ironstone plates.

Jan leaned back, put his hands on his stomach, and smiled. "Good, right?"

Annabel nodded and put her utensils down.

"So where have you been, world traveller?" he asked lightly.

When she didn't answer, he looked at her thoughtfully. He turned himself sideways, bent a long leg, and dropped his boot on the bench. He wrapped his arms around his knee. It seemed as though he now realized he had been inappropriate. That lessened the tension.

"Do you want to hear about my adventures?" he asked.

"What kind of adventures?"

"Just my travels."

"Okay, go ahead." She said it with a warning tone.

As the tentative conversation turned to travel, the timbre of the visit changed. Jan's stories told of interesting and daring journeys. He had been on adventure tours all over the world from safaris in Africa to mountain-climbing in Nepal. Before long, Annabel began to let her guard down. She laughed as heartily as Jan at his various escapades.

Even though his trips had been further afield, she had some interesting travel tales herself. Besides the Netherlands, she had travelled to other European countries, as well as various places in the United States.

The sky above had turned very black and was now filled with stars beyond the countless treetops. The campground was quiet.

Jan looked up after he gulped down more beer from the can in his hand. "Starry, starry night," he said with feeling. "Vincent Van Gogh, my favourite artist. I know all about him."

"I know about him as well." Annabel tipped her head back to gaze at the heavens. "He wanted to be a pastor, I think, but he was turned down by the school that educated them. That's when he went to a mining town to become a lay preacher."

She turned to look at Jan, who was watching her with soulful eyes.

The velvet darkness of night enveloped them. Jan lit the large white candle that was stuck into a low glass jar with melted wax. It glowed from the centre of the table, softening their faces.

"You are so beautiful." Jan looked at her and sighed. "I would love for my brother to meet you. He wouldn't believe I'd met such a beauty."

"What?" She gave a hesitant laugh.

The compliment was nice, but uncomfortable in how he said it. She was used to hearing compliments from Conner, although it had been a while. Not from a stranger. It made her want to go home to her husband, or at least to the relative safety of her car.

"I want to hold you in my arms," he said. "Stay the night with me."

She bit her lower lip. "You're kidding, right?"

"No one will ever know. Stay with me tonight."

"I will know. God will know. I won't cheat on my husband!" she cried out, glad that she hadn't allowed herself to be talked into drinking any alcohol which would have lowered her inhibitions.

"God? What's He got to do with it? It's not cheating if no one knows." His voice was insistent.

"It is cheating, and I'm not interested!" she insisted. "It's late. I'd better go." She signalled toward her campsite with a tilt of her head.

His eyes pleaded. "One kiss first. A goodnight kiss."

"Nope. Sorry. I'm a married woman."

"But you find me as attractive as I find you?"

"I find my husband attractive."

Jan stood. He was a giant akin to the mighty evergreens. Even his shadow appeared ominous. His face wore the night shadows like a dark mask.

He moved his hand toward the dripping candle on the picnic table. "I'll put my hand over this flame, and I won't take it off until you give me that kiss!"

"Like Vincent Van Gogh did over love for his cousin? No. It's not going to happen. Spare yourself the pain. What are you? A dark angel?" she cried aloud.

To herself she thought him not only dark, but insane.

Annabel arose abruptly and started to walk across the road. Then she turned her head to look back and saw that he had removed his hand from the candle.

"You are a good cook," she called. "Thanks for dinner. Enjoy the rest of your stay in the Canadian Rockies."

She hoped she had been curt enough to set a boundary, yet polite enough to be socially appropriate. He said nothing but gave a single wave as he bent to pick up another beer can. Annabel heard the hiss as it opened. He sat atop the table and watched her retreat. He had not had his victory.

Annabel hugged her sleeping puppy beneath her sweater. This wasn't what she had anticipated for her camping trip. She headed for the tent, an intense feeling of anxiety arising in her chest. This time she heeded the insistent warning from her thumping heart.

Sleep in the car, it said.

Quickly she dug the keys out of her jeans pocket and climbed into the passenger side. She locked the door, then stretched out over the two-bucket seats with her sleeping dog placed carefully over her lap. She barely suppressed a shudder as she leaned her head against the cool window.

The glow from Jan's campsite persisted into the night, but at least she was safe in here. Despite the long journey, the disturbing experience, and physical discomfort, Annabel fell into a troubled sleep.

EIGHT

The sharp call of a bird pierced the air and roused Annabel from her dreams. She groaned and tried to stretch in the confined space of the front seat. The wan light of early morning mingled with a gentle mist that enveloped the camp and obscured the trees, tent, vehicles, and structures. She lay there, cold and uncomfortable. Her tent had a cot with a mattress, her sleeping bag, pillows, and a warm wool blanket; she hadn't envisioned starting her camping trip by sleeping in the car.

Annabel reached back with both hands and massaged her neck. She flexed it right and left a few times, pulling down on the sides to deepen the stretch. The mountain air was damp as well as cold, and without a blanket it made her muscles and joints feel tight and sore.

She pulled her sleeping dog close to her face and pressed her mouth into the soft fur. Several tears escaped and rolled down her cheeks. More tears followed until they streamed onto Muffin's fur.

Scenes from the previous night played across the screen of her mind. In her imagination, they resembled a B-rated movie. Feeling confused and humiliated, she wrapped her arms around Muffin in a hug and cried.

"Lord Jesus, I was so foolish," she prayed. "I never should have gone to that man's campsite or eaten at his table. What was I thinking, Lord? It should have been a firm flat-out no. I never should have called Conner except to tell him I had arrived safely. I put Muffin and me in a potentially dangerous situation. Oh Lord, thank You for keeping us safe."

She sniffed back a new onslaught of tears and dug beneath her sweater for the neckline of her T-shirt. She mopped her face with it and drew in a ragged breath.

Once the crying ceased, a semblance of peace enveloped her. She leaned back into its comfort a few minutes before she struggled to move her body into an upright position. She thought again of Conner's warnings about the low nighttime temperatures in the mountains, even in summer. He had been right, as usual.

Annabel pushed the passenger door open and placed Muffin on the seat. She stepped outside and closed the door quietly. The morning mist still hung in the air. Her breath made a faint visible trail as she breathed out. With arms stretched overhead, she lengthened her spine, then twisted to the right and to the left several times. Peace worked its way a bit deeper into her heart.

She gazed around, careful not to look directly at the campsite across the road. Jan was probably passed out considering all the beer he drank. She didn't hear a sound. The other campers were likely still snug in their tents. The glorious silence made her smile, thinking she might be the only one awake. In this moment, the morning and the mountain belonged to her alone.

Annabel hugged her arms around herself. Then she turned to head for the back of the car to get the kettle so she could make tea to warm up.

As she stepped away from the car, something caught her attention. Her head jerked abruptly to the right, and she glanced down at the passenger window. There were clear marks on the foggy window just where her head had been. Five marks. It looked like four fingers and a thumb. There was also a handprint right where she had rested her head… marks that would have fit perfectly over her head!

With an emotional jolt, she tried to process this. She turned to stare at the site across the road. It would have taken a big hand to make a print like that. Jan was tall and muscular and his hands were large. Had he visited her site last night? Had he tried the tent first?

Her stomach heaved. She grabbed the side of the car as her knees buckled. Squatting down, she put her head between her knees and breathed deeply until the lightheaded and nauseous feelings lessened.

Then she stood and leaned back against the car. She continued to stare at Jan's tent.

If it had been Jan, he likely would have been acting under the influence of too much alcohol. And if it hadn't been him? Realistically, who else could it have been? Her emotions became chaotic. Fear fought with logic and anxiety battled against good sense. She had come away to find refreshment and rediscover something valuable in herself, but all she wanted to do was pack up and go home. She felt cheated. She had allowed Jan to jeopardize it all.

Leaving was a good idea. Annabel strode over to the tent, unzipped it, and entered. She stood under the dome. How proud she had been to learn to put the tent up! That feeling seemed a lifetime ago. Bible, journal, pen, pillows, wool blanket… she grabbed the things she had carefully laid out on the cot and took them back to her car. She could pack up the cot and tent once she checked out of the campground.

Even though she opened the door and slammed it shut several times as she rearranged everything inside the hatch and back seat, she didn't seem to notice the noise she made. In her present state of mind, she was oblivious to the fact that she might be disturbing those who wanted to sleep late.

Annabel glanced down at herself. It would feel good to shower and change. But in an instant, she decided not to take the time to do so, even though she had slept in her clothing. It would be easy enough to find a place to change in town.

She glanced at her watch, which had a picture of her pup on it. It was still early, but she wanted out. Now.

The car revved as she drove slowly out of her site. She turned onto the main road and approached the office. She saw no lights on and a sign in the window indicated that the building was still closed.

Disappointed, she proceeded down the road. She would have to check out later, but she wouldn't stay here in the meanwhile.

With intensity, Annabel careened down the winding mountain road to the town site. The main street, lined with restaurants and shops, was nearly empty at this early hour. Only a few vehicles were parked along both sides. She drove to the southern end near the bridge, turned right, and pulled up beside a café across from the park. The red sign in the window announced that it was open. She sighed in relief.

The bell jingled when she pushed on the door. A middle-aged man with greying hair glanced up from the counter where he was arranging baked goods. He studied her dishevelled appearance. Annabel's hand flew to her hair to smooth it down. She hadn't thought to brush it. What a sight her appearance must make.

"Good morning," he greeted her. "You're up early. Or have you just arrived from traveling?"

His diction was clear and his pronunciation precise. He was likely an educated man who had retired to the mountain town.

"Up early to enjoy the fresh air," Annabel replied, making an effort to keep her tone upbeat even though she was fairly certain her pale, unwashed face and rumbled clothing told a different truth.

"Well, what can I get you?"

"English Breakfast tea with the teabag out and a cheese scone, please."

"Did you want butter and jam with the scone?"

"Raspberry jam, if you have it."

"Yes, I can do that."

While he busied himself with her order, Annabel sat on a nearby stool. A heavy sigh escaped before she could press her lips together to suppress it. Her hands moved nervously up and down her thighs.

The man behind the counter glanced at her. "Did you want that to stay or to go?"

"To go, please."

"To go, it is," he said with a smile.

The man's eyes were kind and his words gentle. Somehow, the normalcy of this mundane conversation made her feel out of harm's way for the time being, despite being alone in a café at this early hour.

"Here you go. Tea and a scone. Please be careful. The water is very hot." He handed her a small brown bag and styrofoam cup with a lid. Both had the café's logo on them. "Teabag and jam are in the bag with the scone."

Annabel nodded and paid for the purchase. She thanked the man and wished him a pleasant day. He just leaned on the counter and watched as she exited.

She looked toward her car and saw that Muffin was awake and pawing at the passenger window, whimpering. Annabel put her purchases on the hood of the car, unlocked the door, and lifted her dog into a hug as tears stung her eyes again. This trip was supposed to be about the two of them getting away, about feeling happy and safe. She felt neither.

"Hungry?" she crooned. "I bet you are."

The dog gave a little bark in reply and scrambled onto the front seat as Annabel leaned forward.

Back behind the wheel, she drove further down the street and pulled into the empty parking lot by the beautiful park near the river. She stopped close to a picnic table, then quickly exited the car and rummaged in the cooler for the canned dog food. Once her purchases were laid out on the table, she filled Muffin's bowl and poured some of the hot water from the unmade tea to make gravy to warm it. She set the bowl on the seat of the picnic table. Leash in hand, she led her dog there and lifted her to the seat where the food waited.

Love welled up inside Annabel. She did indeed adore her little companion.

She took her time with the scone and tea. She savoured each bite, allowing the pungent cheese to tickle her tastebuds.

All the while, she looked around. The view in every direction was spectacular and the crisp air exquisite. The varied greens of the forest that surrounded the river and extended up the mountainsides, the expanse of grass crisscrossed by shadows of cooler hues, called to her. The clumps of bushes and rustic wooden boxes of colourful flowers all beckoned. She thought about the sketchbook and coloured pencils in her car. Tempting.

Instead of rushing for them, she continued to take in the setting while stroking Muffin's head. She was glad they were alone in the midst of this natural beauty. She began to reconsider her earlier determination to head for home and abandon her vacation.

"Ought we to go home or stay?" she mused aloud.

Muffin gave a soft bark and thumped her tail.

Annabel laughed softly. "Oh, so you don't want to go home yet?"

Shiny, innocent brown eyes looked up at her. Muffin shook herself and thumped her tail as Annabel cleared up the remains of their breakfast and put the dog dish back in the car. She looked longingly at the art bag, barely visible on the back seat.

She abruptly closed the hatch.

They took the trail that curved north along the river. The landscape God had lovingly created began to work its wonders on the terror and indignation in Annabel's heart. The fear melted away, replaced with calm as they slowly walked along the pathway. She noticed again how the water moved quickly in the opposite direction, creating small caps of white where it paused between the rocks.

By the time they returned to the car, the streets were becoming populated with tourists.

On the walk, Annabel had made a firm decision. She wasn't going to waste either the trip or the day.

Back at her car, she found her toiletries bag and a towel. Then she unzipped her suitcase and grabbed fresh jeans and a blue top with an ivory printed floral design, clean undergarments, and socks. As she headed for the ladies' washroom on the north side of a stone building in the park, her determination began to build. This day was theirs. She would find a way to enjoy it with her dog.

She pushed aside thoughts of Jan from the Netherlands for the time being. She emerged twenty minutes later feeling fresh and clean. All she needed was a plan for the day. In this beautiful place, it couldn't be that hard to make one.

NINE

The Banff Springs Hotel had always been a favourite place for Annabel and Conner. It overlooked the valley she had admired on her way to the campsite the day before, but from a different angle and direction. That hotel was their destination now. There were lovely shops inside with expensive merchandise, and it was fun to window shop to check out fashions and items from around the world. The architecture featured covered alcoves and benches to rest on and enjoy the scenic views. It wasn't likely she would encounter any awkward social situations there, and no one would mind that she had her dog along. It was the perfect place.

It was easy to find a parking spot on the road nearby, as the hour was still early. Annabel grabbed her pink backpack, a gift from Conner. It didn't take long to put in the things they would need for a few hours. Along with her small purse and a lightweight sweater, she carefully placed inside Muffin's covered water dish full of fresh water and a bag of dog treats. She added an apple, a few granola bars, and bottle of water for herself.

She looked longingly at her art bag on the back seat, beside Muffin's carrier. Inside was a high-quality sketchbook, her blue pencil case with professional grade pencils, eraser and sharpener, and the yet-unused set of twenty-four coloured pencils.

She shook her head wistfully and began to turn away, then opened the back door and grabbed the bag before she could change her mind. She stuffed it into her backpack. Taking it along at least gave her the option to draw. That was a step forward, wasn't it?

Instead of going inside the shops, Annabel chose a stone bench in a large covered alcove. She picked up her dog and placed her carefully on the sweater she had laid there; the cold stone wouldn't be comfortable without something to cover it. Muffin curled up with her chin on her paws, watching people with her soulful brown eyes until she fell asleep. Annabel also watched the variety of people as she tried to work up the nerve to start a drawing. She used to favour portraits and figures as subjects. Now it seemed to be a distant memory.

She took a granola bar out of her bag and unwrapped the top. The first bite offered the bittersweet taste of dark chocolate. She took a second bite as she gazed at the beautiful view of the valley and surrounding cliffs.

She was about to reach for the art bag when she was interrupted. A well-dressed couple that looked to be just beyond middle-aged seated themselves nearby. The man heaved himself onto the seat while his wife sat delicately on the edge of it.

"Tired out from hiking?" the heavyset man asked in a gruff voice, rubbing his cheek. He motioned with his fleshy hand toward the dog.

"No, we haven't been hiking yet. I suppose the heat yesterday tired her out," Annabel replied politely even though she wasn't looking for conversation.

"I expect so. It's going to be very hot today, too. Nice and cool on these stone benches, though." He paused. "We're here from the coast. Near Vancouver, to be exact. We're close enough to the ocean to get that nice sea breeze, so it's never as hot there. Where are you from, little lady?"

She replied hesitantly. "I'm from this province."

"City or country? Urban or rural?"

"City."

The man leaned forward on a burnished wooden cane. "Does it have a name?"

"Edmonton."

"Ah." He pulled back and leaned against the wall. "I had a lady friend from Edmonton once. I'll bet she still lives there. Beautiful lady. The wife here met her once, didn't you, Agnes?"

His wife was slender and dressed in an expensive-looking summer outfit. Her brown hair was well-coiffed and her makeup made her plain features more attractive. She looked down at her hands folded on her lap. She nodded without looking up.

"You know, I should call her and see if she'll come to Banff," the man said. "I'd like to see her again. She doesn't drive but she could take a bus. She's a real dish. Gorgeous."

His wife tried to hide the embarrassed expression on her face by turning away to look toward the lovely view to the east. She rubbed her hands together nervously, then fingered a large gold hoop earring.

Annabel looked at the woman with compassion, feeling truly sorry for her. She shouldn't have to listen to her husband gush on about another woman. Hopefully, he wouldn't ruin their vacation by calling his lady friend. Conner would never do such a thing.

The thought made her miss her own husband. She would call him later.

As the man continued his monologue, Annabel nodded absently. Unbidden, her mind excavated thoughts about Jan from the Netherlands. She'd believed she had buried them sufficiently earlier that morning, but she stiffened inwardly as the memories resurfaced and scenes from the previous night began to replay. His comments about her looks had been as unsavoury as this man's commentary on his absent friend.

She saw in her mind the handprint on the car window and again felt the need to escape pressing in on her. Although she had hoped to enjoy this spot for several hours, and perhaps even begin a drawing, the desire to touch her art supplies vanished. Panic moved in and replaced the sense of well-being she had begun to regain.

Annabel pulled her backpack over her shoulder and picked up her dog and sweater. She cleared her throat as she looked for a way to leave gracefully. The man was still expounding upon the virtues of his absent woman friend, oblivious to his wife's quiet humiliation and Annabel's disinterest.

Finally, she just interrupted him. "Well, I hope you folks enjoy your time in this beautiful mountain park," she said with a perkiness she didn't feel.

"What? Oh, yeah. We'll enjoy ourselves. That's what money is for, isn't it?" He guffawed. "Come on, wife, we should go, too. Let's find a phone. I want to call my friend. I'd like to see her again. She's a doll and lots of fun, too."

Annabel walked away, sorry to have lost her spot in the shade. The encounter with that couple had left her in an irritable mood. She knew that if she didn't do something quickly, it would lead to the same old ruts of negativity. But she didn't know what to do next.

It seems I'm becoming a magnet for troubled people, she lamented. *All I want is to be alone with my dog.*

She quickened her pace back toward her car, thinking about relationships and marriages. Muffin, walking on her leash, suddenly tugged to a stop and looked up at her owner. She seemed to be asking why they were hurrying.

Annabel stooped down to pat her head. "I'm sorry, Muffin. I guess I'm letting people get to me. It's wrecking our time together. How about another walk by the river and a picnic in the park?"

Muffin sat up on her back legs and pumped her front paws in the air in excitement. Walk? That was a word she liked!

Annabel laughed. Was psychology really a route she should take? Even though she did have a godly compassion for others, their problems usually made her feel stressed out, especially when she didn't know how to help them. She wondered if there was such a thing as an animal psychologist. Animals seemed easier to understand than people.

By the time they reached her car, the heat had begun to bear down on them. She opened the door and found the interior as hot as an oven, so she rolled down the windows to let the heat escape. She would have to find a shaded place to park in town.

Before driving away, Annabel looked back at the grand hotel they had left. Once more the image of Agnes, the well-dressed woman with the flippant husband, came to mind. Annabel began to wonder what it took to make a happy life. That marriage had felt as stifling as the car before she'd opened the windows.

Would there ever be an open window for Agnes? Or was Agnes herself partly responsible for the way things were?

But it wasn't her problem. Annabel was thankful they weren't her clients; she wouldn't know how to help them. She drove up the road, made a U-turn, and doubled back. Somehow she had to find a way to enjoy the day.

TEN

Even though the parking lot looked full, Annabel circled around until she found a spot in the shade near the old natural history museum. She thanked God for it as she unbuckled her seatbelt. Muffin sat panting on the front seat, eager to get out.

They were walking across the plush grass in minutes. Annabel scanned the park and saw a picnic table in the shade. There were no other tables nearby and this one had a pretty view of the river. She quickened her pace and snagged it before anyone else could get there first.

Her dog needed water and treats, so she attended to that first. She laughed as Muffin slurped up the cool water and took the small tidbits one at a time from her hand. The dog was a good traveller. One of the first things they'd done when Conner brought the dog home was take her for car rides. They took her everywhere now. She was one of the best gifts her husband had ever given her.

Annabel lifted Muffin to the top of the lacquered wooden picnic table. She turned around two or three times, then plopped down with a sigh.

She took out her own snacks next. She opened the bottle of water and took a long drink. She had read somewhere that water was good for settling the nerves and dealing with stress. Whether drinking it, swimming in it, or just sitting next to it, the water was therapeutic—and she had two of the three right there, the water bottle and the river.

Even though the art materials called to her, she didn't respond. They remained in her backpack. Instead she sat silently, pausing from the unwelcome chaos that had found its way into her vacation.

I'll let the water do its magic, she thought. *Then we'll see if art shows up.*

Her thoughts wandered as she watched the flow of the river. Again she considered the wisdom of earning a master's degree in counselling psychology. She wasn't even certain how she had come to apply for the program. It seemed to her that Conner hadn't been satisfied with her achievements; her lack of achievements would have been more truthful. He had told her that she was smart but hadn't gone far enough in her education. Art was merely a hobby. She needed to reach higher. Higher, like his post-doctorate?

Although she believed he meant well, his remarks were scars on her confidence. Her inner landscape had changed when he started to make those comments. Her more positive disposition faded and a moody negativism took root, creating distance between them that didn't necessarily show on the surface. She knew they both felt it with growing bewilderment.

Annabel had increasingly lost her desire to create art. Even when she tried, she never felt it was good enough. Eventually, she just stopped trying and hid the creative part of herself deep inside her heart. The door was locked and she didn't bother to try to find the key anymore. Her art supplies were packed in boxes and bins and stored in the basement of their house.

No wonder Conner thought it was just a diversion. Perhaps, if she could recover her confidence on this trip, he would see things differently. May he would be proud of her, not embarrassed at her limited education. She could begin to sell her work and be a better financial contributor to their household. A more content one, too.

Yet Conner would probably say that she had the summer to do art if she wanted. Grad school was a certainty she ought not to take for granted. There were likely many people who wanted to get into that psychology program, and she had one of the few spots. And he would be correct.

She could feel her shoulders hunched up toward her ears. Her head was down and her lips pressed together into a dismal line. Her right hand grasped the water bottle and the left one clenched into a fist. With alarm, she wondered if she and Conner were more messed up than that couple from the coast.

She took another drink, then put the bottle on the table. Her fingers felt stiff, so she flexed her hands as she lifted her shoulders up and down to release some of the tension. So much for the magic of water! It didn't have the power to stop the thoughts that made her so edgy.

The sun had passed the midday point and begun its descent toward the horizon beyond the mountains. Annabel shifted on the hard wooden seat and glanced at her watch. Thoughts and questions were surfacing, but she had no clarity, no answers. Perhaps she was afraid of those answers.

She squinted up at the sun and then looked down at her hands.

Regardless of why she was doing it, at least Conner seemed happy that she would soon go back to school. She had found something that pleased him. He would no longer disapprove of her, and she wouldn't blame him. She had found the program and applied for it. He had supported her in her application. Any good psychologist would say that she had to take responsibility for her own feelings and choices. She would have to give this advice to many people in the future, if she became a therapist.

Annabel remained confused and conflicted. She felt uncomfortable in her own life. How could it be that she was now too fearful even to pick up a pencil? Hopelessness threatened to take over the day.

"Lord, can you help me, please?" she asked in desperation. "I've asked You so many times."

A thought came to mind and Annabel voiced it aloud.

"Baby steps!" She slapped her hands on her thighs. "Mom believes in taking baby steps for everything. She believes in me. I will try, for her sake as well as mine."

With resolve, Annabel reached for her backpack. She slowly removed the sketchbook and blue pencil case. She chose a sharp 2B pencil and opened to the second page of the book; she never used the first page.

Her head turned to the left and the right as she looked for inspiration. Shadows gave definition to the trees and buildings. There were many choices of subject.

Her eyes alighted on a crooked spruce tree close to the pathway beside the river. It intrigued her. It leaned to one side, its motion captured, forever inert. Pencil to paper, she made the first marks on the page. Something shifted inside her spirit. It was like the doorway to freedom opened a crack.

Two hours later, she held the sketchbook in both hands and flipped the pages. She had filled three of them with drawings: the tree, the river, and a group of people at a table who were visiting and laughing. There was real feeling in the sketches. Emotion! They weren't bland or boring. The range of values emphasized the lights and shadows, giving the drawings life.

She closed the book and sighed with satisfaction before returning her art materials to her backpack. She thanked God for His answer. Her mother's advice remained astute; baby steps can take you somewhere. You just needed the courage and faith to try.

ELEVEN

As they made their way back to the campsite, Annabel mentally arranged plans for the evening. She would call Conner, make supper, and then visit the amphitheatre. Most of all, she would definitely ignore Jan from the Netherlands if he was at his site. This was her vacation. She would make the choices that were best for her and Muffin. For her and Conner. He expected his wife to return happier and less stressed. She hoped she could accomplish it.

"Lord," she prayed, "thank You that the day turned around for the better. I praise You that I was able to draw. It was marvellous, Lord. I feel humbled at the talent You have given me. Forgive me for not using it for so long. Please keep the flow going. So many things can distract me. Discouragement is a big one. Amen."

Annabel pulled around the corner into the camping section with some hesitation. She really didn't want to encounter Jan. Thankfully, no one was at his site—although his tent and high pile of cans told her he would be back. She had no idea where he spent his time, but she didn't care. All she wanted was solitude and peace.

She backed into her own spot and turned off the ignition. Still guarded, she looked around thoroughly before stepping out of the car. There was no one around.

She walked her dog in the opposite direction along the loop road. Tents of many colours waved in a slight breeze like multicoloured flags beneath the tall trees. Every site was rented. Muffin investigated various weeds, bushes, and rocks as they slowly made their way around the circle.

Within ten minutes, they were at the phone booth. Annabel dialled her home number and waited for Conner to pick up. It rang until the answering machine clicked on. Her heart tugged when she heard his voice on the recorded message. The automated operator repeated its message several times, but he wasn't there to accept the collect call.

Annabel hung up and shrugged. He should have been home by now. She would have to try again later.

To celebrate the advent of her new artistic freedom, Annabel laid a cheerful red-and-white-checkered tablecloth on the picnic table. She set the cooler in the shade on one of the attached benches. For safety, she tied Muffin's leash to a table leg while she ate her warmed-up food. Even though her dog was well-mannered and unlikely to run off, Annabel wasn't going to take chances while she was busy making a salad and cheese sandwich for her own supper.

Every now and then, she looked up quickly to make certain there was no one at the table across the road. It was still vacant, for the time being.

The distinct aromas of the mountain aroused her senses. Annabel breathed in with eyes closed, trying to name the scents.

With eyes open, she reached across the table and pulled the amphitheatre program closer to study it. The topic for the presentation tonight was called Wildflowers of the Rockies. She would enjoy that! She loved flowers. Years ago, she had planned to complete a series of miniature paintings of wildflowers. It would be delightful to revisit the idea. She had no concerns about bringing Muffin, so it should be a stress-free outing. The presentation would start just before dark.

Annabel put Muffin in the car so she could clean up the dirty dishes and get ready. She planned to drive and park near the theatre so she wouldn't have to find her way back in the dark alone.

Just before dusk blended into the indigo blue of evening, Annabel and Muffin were seated at the end of a row along the centre aisle between two long sections of benches. The amphitheatre filled up quickly. She deliberately took up more space than was needed, putting her purse and jacket next to her so she wouldn't have to sit too close to anyone. They had come to enjoy the evening.

A nice-looking blonde man approached her row. He looked about Annabel's age.

"Is this seat taken?" he inquired politely, pointing just past Annabel. "I want to be halfway up from the stage."

He looked harmless enough. She indicated that it was free but didn't slide her jacket over to make more room. She kept her purse on the bench with the strap around her arm for safety and to maintain the distance. Muffin sat on her lap.

The man wore designer jeans and an unbuttoned beige cardigan. As he passed in front of her, she smelled the woodsy scent of his aftershave lotion.

Once he was seated, he turned toward her. She noticed the sad expression in his otherwise sultry brown eyes right away and wondered whether he was going to ask her for help of some kind. She held her breath.

"I'm Benjamin. I hope you don't mind my introducing myself to you," he said uncertainly.

"Not at all." She smiled at him. "I'm Annabel and this is Muffin."

Benjamin smiled back and greeted Muffin, who was curled up on Annabel's lap. The dog lowered her head on her owner's arm and looked carefully at the man from under her long eyelashes.

"I'm from Montreal," he said. "This is my first time in the Rockies. Very beautiful."

"You don't have a French accent. Are you certain that's where you're from?" Annabel said with a broader smile.

"Oh, I'm from the English part of Montreal. I'm a veterinarian. I came here because I just broke up with my longtime girlfriend. I thought it would be a good idea to come away by myself." He paused and passed his right hand over his chin and mouth. "Maybe it wasn't such a good idea."

Annabel trapped a sigh before it could escape. This was very personal information to tell a stranger. He definitely seemed needy. She had read that correctly. She was vulnerable herself and had to get things together this week. Once she was trained as a therapist, perhaps she would know how to help people. But all she wanted tonight was to enjoy the presentation.

Another thought occurred to her. Perhaps this man was looking for a way out of his loneliness. She warned herself not to succumb to him. She didn't need any other complications on this trip.

"I'm sorry that happened to you, but I hope you'll still find a way to enjoy yourself here," she said.

"Thank you," he replied with a sad smile. "I will certainly try."

"Enjoy the program," she added in a whisper.

Benjamin leaned close. "I will."

The presentation was about to begin, so they both turned to face the stage. A park ranger stood on the platform and adjusted the microphone. He spoke a few words to test the volume. Annabel then turned her attention to a lowered screen with a projection of flowers on it. The colours were beautiful and she wished she knew the names of the blooms. She had much to learn about wildflowers if she ever hoped to paint them convincingly.

The program passed quickly. The park ranger appeared to know all the varieties of flowers in the area and presented them with insight and good humour. She was glad she had come.

At the conclusion, people applauded before they rose and began to file out.

"Did you like the program?" Benjamin asked her just as he was about to walk away.

She responded with an enthusiastic thumbs up. He returned the gesture using both hands.

He seemed like a nice man. She wished she could help him in some way without jeopardizing herself or Muffin, but she realized it would only take more time away from her ability to recover her art. Yet the lines of his pleasant face and the expression in his sad eyes would also make him an interesting subject for a portrait. She wondered if she should ask him to sit for her.

She smiled to herself. What would she rather do, help him or paint him? She really didn't know the answer.

Seeing a break in the line of people moving up and out of the outdoor theatre, Annabel entered the upwardly slanted aisle. Benjamin exited right behind her.

As they walked away from the stage, he said something to her, but his words were lost in the noise of the crowd. When she turned her head to ask him to repeat it, her gaze wandered and she saw Jan from the Netherlands, standing alone, watching her intently. Her heart sank. She didn't want to talk to him.

She looked away quickly, hoping that he hadn't realized she had seen him. Her hope was in vain, though. By the time she reached the top of the aisle, he had moved in beside her.

"You weren't around today."

Annabel didn't reply. Her heartbeat picked up pace, and she

tried not to let emotion take over.

"I waited this morning to see if you would return," he said a little louder.

"There was no need for you to do that." She didn't make eye contact. She didn't want anyone to think there was something between them.

Benjamin touched her back lightly and she turned enough to see his face. He mouthed, *Do you need help?* Annabel nodded slightly.

Her new acquaintance moved in between the two of them. "Annabel, I will see you to your car as I promised."

Benjamin placed his right hand firmly on her back to propel her forward. Annabel clutched Muffin tightly as she walked away, leaving Jan behind.

"Will you be okay getting back to your site?" Benjamin asked when they reached her car.

"I'll be fine now," she assured him.

There were question marks all over his face. Although he could see she was clearly shaken by the intrusion of the tall blonde man, he was gentleman enough not to ask her for an explanation.

She forced herself to smile. "Long story and not worth telling."

"I'm in the young people's tenting area, in site number 21, if you need anything." He sounded sincere and concerned. "I have a rental car."

Not only was he in the same section, she realized, but he was quite near. She nodded and smiled her thanks, revealing nothing.

She considered offering him a ride but decided against it. One complication had already been enough nearly to ruin her vacation.

"That's kind of you," she said. "I'll keep that in mind."

Benjamin walked off after she locked the car doors and started the car. She headed out of the parking lot and onto the main road.

She knew she could beat Jan back, if she hurried.

When she pulled in beside her site, her neighbour wasn't yet at his tent. She drove further on to the washhouse. No way would she walk there in the dark tonight, but she had to get ready for bed. It was a blessing that her toiletry bag was in the car.

Back at her site, she stood beside her tent and tried to work up the nerve to open the zippers and go inside. She couldn't do it. She made a quick turn and instead walked back to her car. With a quick motion, she grabbed the blanket and a pillow from the hatch and slammed it shut.

Instead of sleeping on her comfortable camp cot, she settled herself on the front passenger seat with her feet on the driver's side. Muffin nestled beside her with her head on Annabel's lap. She put her arm around the little dog. It certainly was a humble bed, but she felt safer in the car with the key ring around her finger. She could leave easily and quickly enough if she had to do so.

As Annabel drifted off to sleep, she realized that she had forgotten to call Conner. Even though she was concerned that he might be worried, she didn't want to walk back to the payphone in the dark—and it didn't make sense to drive there this late. The call would have to wait until morning.

Night enfolded her in its soothing arms. She heard voices and laughter as people returned to their tents, but Annabel refused to turn her head to see if Jan was there, although she suspected he would be seated on top of the picnic table with another can in his hand, watching her site.

With a deep sigh, she let sleep take over and hoped she wouldn't have troublesome dreams.

She knew she could beat Jan back if she hurried.

When she pulled up [illegible] the door, [illegible] No way would [illegible] she had to get ready [illegible] to the car.

Back [illegible] Beside [illegible] and [illegible] she [illegible]

Instead of [illegible]

TWELVE

The bear was rummaging through a garbage can. It dropped the can to the ground and turned toward her site. The beast ambled through the brush, its great bulk knocking off twigs and flattening the foliage as it moved toward the spot where she stood. Annabel tried to scream but no sound came out. The bear came closer and closer, and as it did its hairy face transformed into the visage of Jan from the Netherlands. Next, the body reconfigured into Jan's tall, muscular figure. As he drew near, he reached out to grab her with both of his large hands. Annabel couldn't move. She couldn't escape. When he opened his mouth and began to roar, her tongue loosened. Loud and far-reaching, over and over she screamed.

A noise outside the car awakened her. Annabel opened her eyes wide, panting as she tried to take in enough air. Her forehead was beaded with perspiration despite the cold. Muffin was still asleep with her head on her lap. The wool covering was twisted and half-draped over the floor. She pulled the blanket over her little dog first and then over her own head. It had been a terrifying nightmare.

How Annabel wished Conner had come with her or that she was home in her own bed with her husband. She wanted to leave now. Why had she insisted on coming all by herself anyway? At the least she ought to have listened to Conner and stayed at a motel. She wanted his love and protection. By herself, comfort eluded her. She was too overwhelmed even to cry.

"Calm down," she ordered herself as she buried her face in her dog's long, soft hair. "It was just a dream. You've always had vivid dreams. Things will look differently in the morning."

The positive self-talk didn't work. The fear didn't subside, and anxiety joined it to torment her further. She could think of nothing to do about it in the middle of the night; she had to wait until morning.

She squeezed her eyes shut and tried to force herself to go back to sleep. With her eyes closed, the image of the bear loomed large, along with the leering grin on Jan's face.

She opened her eyes again. Her whole body was in a state of unyielding vigilance. Dreams had meaning and the meaning of this one seemed clear. Prayer was the only thing available to her at the moment, but all she could manage was one word.

Help.

Then another word came to mind: journal. Her journal was precious to her. It was a record of her life, but it also helped to process her feelings and thoughts. It was on the back seat, though, and she didn't know if she could get the book without waking her dog. If Muffin awoke, she would likely need a relief break, and Annabel didn't want to leave the relative safety of her car.

She considered the dilemma for a few minutes before understanding what to do. If she reached behind to lower the seat back as far as it would go and leaned forward, slowly twisting her body, it would allow her left arm the maximum reach.

On the first try, she missed the journal. The second time, she stretched further and was able to grab the corner of the book and inch it forward until she had a firmer grasp. The blue ballpoint pen was stuck in the coil binding. She was careful not to dislodge it.

Annabel opened the book to the last entry. She hadn't written so far on this trip, even though writing was usually part of her daily routine. She scanned the words she had last penned. They expressed enthusiasm and excitement about going to the mountains.

She tapped the pen lightly on the page. At this moment she felt truly alone, but it wasn't the kind of solitude that brought insight, deeper connection, or peace. She felt defenceless and vulnerable. It was all so different than she had anticipated.

She inhaled and slowly exhaled as she placed the pen on the lined sheet. What came out was a prayer she hadn't been able to put into words.

> Lord, Lord, I'm so afraid. Your perfect love casts out fear. Take away this terror. I came away to be at peace, not in distress. I thought I would find the answers I need and some assurance of the direction I'm heading. Forgive me if I shouldn't have come here. Maybe Conner was right. I'm too fragile to be alone, surrounded by strangers. I'm tissue paper torn by the wind. If I'm this vulnerable, how could I ever help anyone else? Show me what to do, the right decisions to make. I can't find the answers, Lord. I don't know what to do. I'm just confused. Please bring me clarity. Keep us safe. Amen.

She reread her entry, then prayed it again and closed the book. She lay perfectly still in the darkness, exhaustion weighing her down. If she left in the morning, her vacation would be over and she would return home. Nothing would have changed. In fact, she might feel even worse. When would she have time again to get herself together before heading to university? Time to figure things out?

The truth was that she wouldn't. Life would continue on as it had before. She would leave her internal artist up in these mountains. It felt like this had been her last chance to redeem that side of her. She tried to discern the answers she needed but detected no clear direction.

In this overwrought, fatigued state, darker thoughts entered her mind. Thoughts about Conner. About their marriage. She wondered where he was tonight and why he hadn't answered the phone. Questions plagued her. Why had he suggested that she come away all by herself without him? Had he wanted to be rid of her? When was the last time he had told her she was beautiful? She was a free spirit, an artist, even if she hadn't been actively practicing her art. Why couldn't he just accept her as she was? Was she really so deficient in his eyes? Why was he forcing her to go to grad school? Did she even want to go? What did she want?

These questions gave voice to her internal fears, but she arrived at no answers. She pondered these thoughts until her eyelids grew heavy and sleep overtook her.

The first signs of daybreak appeared as the sky lightened to a milky blue. Darkness melted into dawn, and dawn gave way to morning. The sun pushed through the heavy foliage.

Annabel opened her eyes partway and squinted at the brightness. She peered at her watch. It was nearly nine o'clock and the car was getting warm. Reaching behind her, she rolled the window down. The fresh morning air rushed in.

It was Tuesday, her third day here. She wriggled from beneath the wool blanket and sat upright. Muffin was fully awake and staring at her. Annabel rubbed the dog's head and snapped on the leash. She then rolled the window up, leaving just a crack for air at the top. In minutes, she was walking her dog through the long, narrow campsite. She headed for the phone booth that lay just around the bend in the road.

She dialled her home phone number and followed the automated instructions. Conner was likely at work, but he would be able to see that she'd tried to call.

Surprisingly, he answered and accepted the collect call.

"Conner!" she exclaimed. "What are you doing home at this hour?"

"Waiting for you to call. I let work know that I would be in late today." There was anxiety in his tone. "Why didn't you call back last night? I've been worried sick about you!"

"Where were you when I called yesterday?"

"Cutting the lawn."

She hung her head, ashamed of the suspicious thoughts and questions that had attacked her emotions last night.

"Oh, Conner, I'm so sorry. I went to the amphitheatre presentation, and it was too dark to walk to the phone booth afterward."

"You could have called earlier. And it's a strange hour to call now," he added, sounding peeved.

"I know. I slept in, and I guess I just lost track of time yesterday." Annabel didn't want him to know about the troubles she had faced. "I got lost in my sketching in the park by the river. And there was a really nice presentation on wildflowers in the evening that I didn't want to miss. I'm sorry, Conner."

"It's okay. Please try to understand that I worry about you and Muffin being out there alone."

"I do understand. Muffin is fine. She's having a great time." To herself, she added, *Better than me.*

"I never should have suggested it or let you go." His voice grew louder. "Why don't you just pack up and come home?"

Annabel didn't know what to say. Even though she wanted the same thing, she began to feel defensive about her trip. He didn't believe she was capable of a few days camping up here alone? Well, she wanted to prove him wrong. He hadn't praised or encouraged her when she mentioned sketching. He didn't appreciate her art; he just expected her to go to grad school.

The same old irritation began to replace her remorse.

Conner sighed audibly when she didn't reply. "Look, sunshine, I have to get to work. I'm glad you're okay. Stay if you want."

She could tell by the tone of his voice that he was likely looking at his watch and regretting lost time at work. She waited a moment longer before she replied.

"Conner," she said hesitantly. "I miss you."

"I miss you, too, sunshine."

She heard the click as her husband hung up. For a few minutes, she stood there holding the earpiece in her hand with its stiff metal cord looped in the air. Then she hung it back in place and turned toward her site.

Annabel had not even slept in the tent, but she didn't want to admit that to her husband. She couldn't go back to the city yet. It would be admitting defeat without giving it a solid try. That was against everything her parents had taught her.

In the full light of day, the situation didn't look as frightening and hopeless. Annabel was glad she had waited until morning to make her decision.

Walking slowly, she hatched what she perceived was a workable plan. She would go to the park office and pay for the rest of the week. That would give her more time to sort things out. Time to try to understand what was really beneath her negative reactions, and also time to explore more of her artistic self to see what might emerge. Things had gotten complicated, but she could work harder to keep the unnecessary complications at bay.

When they reached the picnic table, Muffin shook herself twice and placed her front paws against her owner's legs to stretch as she waited to be picked up. Annabel lifted her and put her face nose-to-nose with the dog.

"I need a shower!"

Muffin gave a little bark. Annabel grabbed her toiletries bag, a towel, and some clean clothing. They headed toward the washhouse where there were two shower cubicles. Thankfully, the larger one with the long bench inside was available.

Muffin jumped up and settled onto the bench right away. Annabel tied the leash to the door handle of the shower room for added safety, although the space under the door was low, it was high enough for the dog to wriggle out if tempted.

She hung her towel on a wall hook and reached in to turn on the shower to warm it. Next, she stepped out of the clothes she had slept in and slipped her feet into thongs. She wouldn't go into a public shower barefoot. Carefully, she placed her garments onto the remaining wall hooks before entering the cubicle.

Steam began to fill the air. The stream of warm water pelted down on Annabel's skin and she raised her head to let it wash over her face. Every cell in her body whispered thankfulness. She scrubbed until she felt totally clean. With her hair washed, she felt renewed and refreshed.

Putting on clean clothes was almost a spiritual experience. She was ready to face another day in the mountains.

At the sink, she combed and braided her long wet hair, then twisted the braids into a bun that she secured with gold-coloured hairpins. She brushed her teeth with mint-flavoured toothpaste and ran her tongue over their smooth surface. She applied minimal makeup—eyeliner, mascara, and a light peach lip balm. Her appearance in the mirror seemed attractive, but her eyes looked weary despite the cosmetics. It would have to be a calm, non-physical day.

After she fed her dog, Annabel gulped down the last of her tea, now lukewarm, and finished the second half of the bagel she had spread with peanut butter.

It occurred to her that she hadn't called her mother. It wasn't that she had promised to do so, but she usually checked in when she travelled. Besides, she just wanted to hear her mom's voice.

She put Muffin in the car before she dashed back to the phone booth with a handful of change. Once her mother answered, the operator requested a deposit of the amount needed for the first three minutes. Annabel quickly dropped in the coins.

"Mom, it's me," she said breathlessly.

"How are you and Muffin making out up there in the mountains?"

Annabel hesitated, which she knew could alert her mother to trouble. "It's not the same being here without Conner, Mom."

"I would imagine so."

Her mother was the considerate and non-intrusive type. She waited for Annabel to continue.

"I sketched yesterday. A tree, the river, and some people."

"How did that go?"

"Really well, Mom. I enjoyed it so much."

"I've always said that art is your identity, not just a hobby. I hope you keep on enjoying it." Her voice oozed enthusiasm.

The operator's voice interrupted and requested more coins for the next three minutes. Annabel squeezed in a few more words before they were cut off.

"I'll try. Well, Muffin is in the car and it's getting pretty warm here."

"You'd better get back to her then. Thanks for calling and letting me know you're safe."

"I love you, Mom."

"I love you, too."

Annabel hung up the phone and walked back to her site thoughtfully. She was glad she had called her mother. It had given her the emotional boost she needed. She would definitely renew her camping permit and see what the day held.

THIRTEEN

At the far end of Banff Avenue, on the east side of the road, stood a bookstore that also sold art supplies. Annabel rounded the corner and parked near the two-story building. She slung her purse over her left shoulder and carried Muffin under her right arm as she climbed the steps.

Just inside the door, she paused. The elderly woman behind the counter looked her way.

"Is it okay if I carry my dog in?" Annabel asked with a little smile. "I'll only be a few minutes and she's very well-behaved."

The grey-haired clerk tilted her head. "Yes, for a short time. Is there something I can help you find?"

She reminded Annabel of a schoolteacher. Perhaps she was a retired educator, but it felt too intrusive to ask a stranger about her past.

"Watercolour paints and accessories."

"The art supplies are behind the pillar to your left. There's a sale bin as well, if you're interested."

Annabel nodded and headed in that direction. It was a tempting environment. The shelves were beautifully arranged with an array of art materials. She found tubes of watercolour paints, brushes, portable water dishes, and specialty papers. The prices were higher than her favourite art store in the city, but she had brought nothing with her except pencils and coloured pencils. She needed watercolour supplies. Touching them sent a thrill through her body, like an electrical current.

She stepped over to the sales bin and began rummaging through it. To her surprise, she discovered a watercolour travel set that included everything she would need. It even had a sketchbook with cold-pressed paper. The paint was of a professional quality, not student grade. And it was marked to half-price.

She snatched it up and carried it to the counter.

"Good choice," the clerk said. "We only had one of those. I had it on hold for someone, but she didn't come back before closing last night."

Annabel beamed. "I'm blessed today!"

She paid with her credit card and left feeling excited about her purchase. God must have led her here at the right time.

Next, instead of staying in town, Annabel drove toward the Trans-Canada Highway. She continued north until she saw a sign that indicated a hiking area. She signalled right and turned onto a winding road.

She had never explored this trail and didn't know what to expect, but she encountered a good parking spot in dense shade that would keep her car cool for the day. She pulled in, shut off the car, and set the parking brake. With her backpack full of water, snacks, a fleece blanket, and her art supplies, she walked her dog across the parking lot and onto the grass.

They headed toward a line of spruce trees that bordered a pristine lake. It was the blue-green colour of so many mountain lakes in the area, crystal clear to the bottom. Breathtaking.

Annabel stopped at the first empty picnic table, positioned half in the shade and half in the sun. She unfolded the blanket and laid it on the bench for her dog. Then she slid herself onto the wooden seat and took out the watercolour kit, removing the plastic wrap.

She set the contents on the table and focused on the watercolours themselves. It was a twelve-colour set in a bright white container. She snapped it open and marvelled at the beauty of the tubes of paint. The set also contained an extendible silver brush with sable bristles. She stroked it with longing in her heart. Her fingers tingled with excitement knowing that soon she would have the brush loaded with paint.

It only took a few minutes to set the sketchbook at a slight angle and fill the small collapsible container from her water bottle. She put it to the right of the paper. With a pause and a deep breath, she withdrew the box that held the precious pigments.

She picked up the first tube. Cadmium Yellow Medium. She squeezed a small amount of this rich primary colour onto the side of the circular ceramic palette. Lemon Yellow. Alizarin Crimson. Ultramarine Blue. One by one, she took the caps off each tube and placed the colour on the edge of the palette. Reverently, she replaced the caps each time and put the tubes in their respective places. It was a ritual she had almost forgotten. The empty wells of the palette awaited the watercolour washes that would eventually lead to the creation of her first painting in a long time.

Annabel paused to look up at the lake. It wasn't hard to find inspiration; it lay all around her, a feast for the eyes.

And then, without warning, her confidence faltered. She questioned herself. Was she still an artist? The anxiety started in the centre of her chest, making her heart flutter. She began to breathe faster. Her vision blurred. She clutched the edge of the table, feeling lightheaded.

I… I can't do it…

She turned sideways and lowered her head between her knees. She breathed slowly, in and then out, over and over again. Even though it was still morning, the early heat of the day felt oppressive.

"I have to go," she said frantically. "I have to leave this place!"

Gradually, she sat upright and looked around her. The panic began to subside as the realization that this was just an ordinary day penetrated her emotions. Although it wasn't crowded, there were people around. A young couple pushed a baby carriage along the path toward her. They were laughing and holding hands. An elderly couple strolled in the opposite direction. Several of the picnic tables were now occupied by small groups of people who had set up to enjoy the day.

A movement to her right caught her attention.

"Hey!" yelled a teenaged boy. A large gull had swooped down and grabbed the bright red ballcap from his head. He chased the bird across the grass, shouting. It then dropped the hat and flew off. The boy grabbed it and shook his fist at the disappearing white creature. He put the hat back on and pulled the front of his oversized flannel shirt closed in indignation as he stalked off.

Any other day, the debacle would have made her laugh, but today she just stared at the scene in disbelief. Yet these diversions shook her out of what might have been a full-blown panic attack.

She turned her eyes back to the picnic table and started to pack her art materials. It had been an expensive mistake buying the watercolour set. It was better just to leave. She would go to grad school as Conner wanted. She was no longer the artist she had once thought she was.

She paused again and beheld the beauty all around. At least she had the memory of being in this place. But she ought to have left for home that morning and not renewed her tenting site. This was all just a big mistake.

Then her mother's message echoed through her mind, those words spoken with love. They were so clear that her mother might as well have been standing right beside her: *"I've always said that art is your identity, not just a hobby. I hope you keep on enjoying it."*

"Mom," Annabel said faintly. Tears filled her eyes and began to drip down her cheeks. She hung her head in remorse. Her parents had raised her never to give up, yet that's exactly what she had done. Quit the very thing that had meaning for her.

Trying to recover her art was harder than she had anticipated.

She leaned her elbows on the picnic table with her cheeks nestled in her hands and gazed across the lake. How had she become so disconnected from the artist inside? If that was her identity, she didn't know who she was anymore.

Muffin whimpered and pushed her head onto Annabel's lap. She stroked the dog's head but kept her eyes fixed on the scene in front of her.

With a heavy sigh, her heart reached for God, and she felt Him reach back. An inexplicable peace surrounded her, and she knew she had to give it another try. She would do it for her mother, even if she couldn't do it for herself. Her wonderful mom, who believed in her creative talents when no one else did.

Most of all, she would do it for the Lord.

She took out some treats for Muffin and got her resettled in the remaining shade. Taking another deep breath, she closed her eyes and swallowed the lump in her throat. Her hands trembled when she replaced the contents of the watercolour kit on the table and resumed her preparations. It was just short of terrifying to take the number four-sized brush in hand, swirl it in the water, and blot it on a tissue.

There was a small island a short distance from the shoreline. Three trees grew on it amid the tall grass, like friends holding hands. Mountains surrounded them in all directions. The sky was light blue. The water shimmered with the sun's illumination.

Annabel dipped the brush into the water and deposited a few large drops into several of the palette wells. Next, she dropped some cool red into one of the puddles of water and mixed it with warm blue to create a rich violet. More crimson made red-violet, whereas blue-violet needed more ultramarine. Lemon Yellow with ultramarine made brilliant greens she could dull with the red. Crimson and yellow created the correct range of oranges. She played with the colours, fascinated anew with colour-mixing experiments.

Finally, she decided on a tertiary colour harmony for the painting. It was slightly annoying that the heat dried the paint so quickly, yet she was soon lost in the process.

The next few hours passed quickly as she became engrossed with layering colour on colour to create glazes that slowly formed the scene. She had always been methodical in her technique.

Annabel paused to scrutinize her efforts. The sun had moved westward, shifting the shadows to different places. It was one of the perils of painting on location.

Only when she reached over and touched Muffin's nose, finding it hot and dry, did she realize that she had been totally mesmerized. Quickly she got the water dish out and apologetically held it for her pup. Treats followed.

Annabel hated to leave the gorgeous location, but it was simply too hot for Muffin, even in the shade.

She looked at the lovely painting she had created. It was as though she had never quit, and she never wanted to stop again. It had been worthwhile to find this place, and even more valuable to find the courage that had led to this moment of triumph.

Annabel closed the sketchbook and held it against her heart. She had believed she had lost the gift of creating art, but she still had it. Today had been enough to convince her.

But now it really was time to pack up her things. She ran her hand over the cover of the sketchbook and looked up to heaven.

"Thank you," she whispered.

She loaded her backpack and retraced her steps to the parking lot. The car was cool because of the dense shade created by the multitude of towering trees. Annabel rolled down the front windows, realizing that she hadn't eaten anything since breakfast.

She reached for her backpack and pulled out an apple. The first bite into the crisp fruit made her tastebuds explode with the flavour. It wasn't physical hunger; somewhere deep within she felt her senses awakening. She closed her eyes and savoured each bite, feeling alive, even more so than when she had sketched the day before.

Muffin crawled onto her lap and she hugged the dog fiercely. Love welled up inside her.

By the time they were back on Banff Avenue, clouds had moved in from the west and obscured the late afternoon sun. Annabel turned right before the bridge. Again, she pulled into the parking lot of the park near the river, just as large drops of rain began to splat against the windows. People fled to their cars, scampered into nearby shops, or took shelter under the roof of the park's outdoor theatre.

Vehicles began to flow out of the area, leaving ample choices for parking. She selected one facing south near the old museum and pulled to a stop. Rolling down the windows just enough to let in the cooling air, she lowered her seat and let herself lean back. The rain drummed against the roof and streamed down the windows. She felt cocooned in the safety of her car.

The rain finally slowed its cadence until its sound was a mere pitter-patter. Annabel fell into a light sleep, breathing in harmony with the rain's music.

When she finally yawned, awake again, the sky was losing light. With surprise she realized that she had napped for longer than expected. It was time to return to the campground.

She turned on the headlights to combat the gloomy dusk, then pulled out of the parking lot and waited at the traffic light. Along the main street, the interior lights of the businesses shone brightly. The neon signs created streaks of colour on the wet pavement.

Annabel rubbed her eyes and yawned again. She pulled up beside a fast food restaurant and got a tea to go—with the teabag out, of course—so she could make Muffin's supper quickly. She wasn't very hungry, so her uneaten lunch would be enough for her.

It was already damp and the air was cooling quickly. They would sleep in the car again tonight. It was too late to fuss with blankets, pillows, and a sleeping bag. Tomorrow would be another day. Perhaps she would finally sleep in the tent.

FOURTEEN

Annabel awoke refreshed the next morning. The sun was barely poking through the branches when she went to wash up for the day. She had avoided looking at Jan's campsite last night. All was quiet there now. Had he left and decided to abandon his tent? She knew that was wishful thinking. It made her feel safer that she hadn't seen him around, but she hadn't been at her site much either.

Low-sugar cereal topped with strawberry yogurt and a banana made a quick breakfast. As she ate, she thought back to her painting time the previous day. She'd been so lost in the moment that nothing else had seemed to exist. Could it be like that again, or had her experience been specific to that moment of time? She wouldn't know unless she kept on taking baby steps back toward recovering her creative self.

The watercolour set had turned out to be a wise purchase after all. Of course, she had her own travel art kit at home with a variety of carefully chosen materials. When she had made the sudden decision to come here, there had been no time to find it. She'd thought it was packed away in a bin but wasn't entirely certain where. When she got home, she would find it and keep it handy. They had a spare room that was rarely used. She determined to set it up as a studio. Certainly Conner wouldn't mind lugging up her old drafting table and art supplies. She would purchase a small easel as well. Thinking about it made her smile.

People emerged from their tents, bundled in jackets or sweaters as barriers to the cool, humid morning. The nearly cloudless sky promised a warm day, so she knew they would all shed the layers later. Their conversation and laughter created a pleasant backdrop. She watched several people walk their dogs, as she had done earlier.

There was still no sign of movement or sound at Jan's site. Annabel took another sip of tea as she glanced across the road. Everything in her hoped that he had left for good. But one thing was definite: no one had cleared up the piles of cans, nor did anyone seem interested in taking them.

Annabel pulled her light green waterproof jacket closed and zipped it shut. Sipping her hot drink, she thoughtfully considered the day that lay before her. She was certain she would be painting again, but she didn't know where to go. She had heard there were beautiful gardens behind the national park offices. That would be a suitable destination. The rain had freshened everything, so it wouldn't seem as hot as it had been earlier in the week. The flowers and vegetation would be revived as well.

Since she had never been to these gardens, she would have to ask for directions on her way.

She found herself emotionally in a better place. She didn't feel as out of sorts and overwhelmed by life. The act of painting had helped. She pulled her Bible toward her and read that the steadfast love of the Lord never ceases; it is new every morning. She closed her eyes and let the words sink deep into her spirit. The passage brought her comfort.

She finished her tea and rinsed the cup with bottled water, using a paper napkin to dry it.

"Well, Muffin, are you ready for another car ride and a new adventure?"

The little dog wagged her tail across the ground as she gazed up into her owner's eyes.

"I promise I won't roast you in the sun today, little girl."

As she turned out of the campground, Annabel decided to take a different route through Banff. She headed left at the bottom of the steep descent toward the town instead of following her usual direction to the right. There were new houses on these residential streets among the quaint older homes that had been there for decades. Some rich and famous people apparently owned property here, but she didn't see anyone in their yards.

She headed across Banff Avenue and slowly toured the streets on the west side before crossing the bridge and followed the curve of the road southward. At the far side of a large building was a sign for the national parks headquarters. Ahead was a nearly empty parking lot. She found the spot that promised the most shade and pulled in.

With her backpack on and dog leash in her right hand, they crossed the lot. The beginning of the gardens was just beyond the lot. Even from a distance, a pleasant mix of floral scents carried toward her on a gentle breeze. She breathed in the heady aroma. Being alone yesterday had brought back her heightened sense of wellbeing and feeling of safety. She hoped today would be even better.

They strolled up the pathway, with manicured lawns surrounding them on every side. Gardeners were busy pruning and planting in the coolness of the morning.

Annabel didn't know where to go first, so she followed the path up some steps. She admired the well-groomed flowerbeds and colourful blooms. The hues were spectacular, and once again she wished she knew more about flowers. She could only name the easier ones, like roses, petunias, and daisies.

As they continued to walk, a thought occurred to her. If she put in the effort, she might be able to get work as a botanical illustrator someday. Illustration had been another childhood dream. Perhaps it wasn't too late to fulfill it in some way. In this lovely place, anything seemed possible.

"I think I'll find a place to sketch flowers," she mused aloud as she turned her head, scanning the area. A covered bench nearby appealed to her. If more rain came, it would provide shelter. And if the sun grew hot, it would give them shade. The stone bench was wide enough for her supplies.

Once they were settled, Annabel lifted her backpack to her lap. She opened it to discover an unpleasant surprise. Her new watercolour kit wasn't inside, only the sketchbook and coloured pencils tucked into the wide inside pocket. She rummaged through the bag. The fleece blanket took up a good portion of the space. There was water, lunch, snacks, and the usual things her dog needed. Her purse was tucked underneath a light sweater.

Disbelief flooded her.

"What in the world?" she exclaimed. "Where did my paint set go?"

The familiar irritability began to arise, along with an unhealthy dose of negativity. It still didn't seem to take much to pull her mood down. She put her hand to her forehead and puffed out an impatient sigh. Tapping her palm against her head, she willed herself to think where the kit might be.

I put it back inside yesterday. I know I did. When would I have taken it out of the backpack? she asked herself with a sour expression that marred her pretty features. She couldn't recall doing so.

She looked up and noticed an approaching figure. Around the curve in the path, a gentleman moved along slowly. He leaned heavily on a gnarled wooden walking stick. His full hair was white as cotton wool, his complexion ruddy, but his face had almost no wrinkles. The man must have been very handsome in his youth. He smiled up at her, but she just stared back at him.

"Good morning," he said pleasantly.

Annabel sighed and remembered her manners. "I hope you are having a pleasant one. Morning, I mean," she replied, trying to keep her voice from sounding as disagreeable as she felt.

"Yes, thank you. A lovely morning, indeed. My my, it doesn't look like you're having one. A good morning, I mean." He wore a hint of a smile and his voice was soft and full of compassion. "Is there anything I can do to help?"

She dropped her hands to her lap. Tears lined the bottoms of her eyes and threatened to leak out. She tried as hard as she could not to cry.

There was another stone bench across from Annabel and the gentleman lowered himself slowly onto it using his stick for support.

"Would you mind if I sat a while here?" he asked.

"Not at all." After all, it was a public park. Anyone could sit anywhere they liked.

He looked to his right at the beautifully planted gardens. "I come here every day. I like to walk in the gardens in the cool of the morning. What about you?"

"It's my first time."

"And you don't like it here?" He raised his thick white eyebrows.

Annabel looked at the gentleman. He seemed genuinely concerned. "I like it very much. It's lovely," she said in a low voice.

"May I be inquisitive and ask why such a beautiful young lady would look so unhappy in a location she likes so much?"

Annabel felt a bit annoyed at the way he repeated parts of what she had said. It wasn't his business to ask personal questions, nor did she have to answer. She looked away from the man and then turned back to face him. The burden of disappointment weighed heavily on her. It seemed to be some kind of a sign, and she didn't want to guess what the meaning might be.

"Well, I came here to sketch and seem to have lost my art supplies. A set of watercolour paints, to be exact." With a weak smile, she added, "That's what's making me unhappy."

He studied her face a moment. Annabel momentarily wished he had the answer to her present dilemma. Even more, she hoped he might have the answer to all her troubles, but that didn't seem very likely.

"Do you recall the last time you had them? Sometimes that helps to jog the memory."

She shook her head as she pulled her mouth to the side, revealing a dimple. "I'm camping, and I don't remember taking the supplies out of my backpack. They were new. I just bought them yesterday." She looked down at her hands, which lay idle in her lap.

"So you're an artist?"

She shrugged.

"Without the tools to create the art?" he continued, looking at her with empathy.

"I'm not really an artist..."

"I see. And is that why the absence of your tools makes you so unhappy?"

Annabel looked up at him intently.

He continued on, sounding as wise as a sage yet with a sparkle in his eyes. He leaned both hands over the knob of his walking stick. "God has a unique plan for each of us. It's our job to discover and use the talents He gave us. It's very easy in life to take a lesser path. To bury a talent and not develop it. Life offers many distractions, and some of them are dangerous." He looked up toward the sky, but then his eyes returned to her face.

Listening, she nodded slightly.

"We are put on the earth for a purpose, but we can miss it," he said. "We can miss the crowning glory God has for us. Do you believe this?"

She looked down at the path a moment, then met his eyes again. "I never thought of that. I think I might be missing out on my purpose. I don't know. I'm not certain what I should be doing in life."

"May I venture to say that this art thing sounds meaningful to you, in my estimation?"

She nodded thoughtfully and looked at the ground again, wondering whether she dared broach the subject of grad school. What would he say?

Annabel was about to take the conversation in that direction when the man spoke again.

"Don't despair. God has an answer for you. If you can take the advice of an old man, don't stop looking for it, and please don't let life's sideshows keep you from the main event. There's the wheat you harvest, but you just let the chaff blow away. Why don't you go back to your camping site? Perhaps you left your new art materials there."

Annabel was going to argue and say something cynical. Instead she closed her backpack and shrugged it over her shoulder. She didn't know much about the harvest, but she did want her watercolour supplies back.

"I will take your advice, sir. Thanks so much."

"We don't always know what's in our hearts. Sometimes God sends experiences to reveal it. The right things come at the right time. We just have to be wise enough to recognize them. You'll find your painting supplies. Keep the faith. All the best in your art making, Annabel."

They both rose at the same time. The gentleman headed back in the direction he had come from.

Annabel gathered Muffin into her arms and took a few steps along the pathway. When she looked back to wave at the gentleman, he was gone.

Then it struck her. He had called her by name. How had he known her name? She hadn't told him. She shook her head and continued to walk.

As she walked, a familiar phrase from the Bible came to mind: *"some people entertain angels unaware."* Is that what had happened?

Regardless, she would follow his advice. Back to the campsite, it would be.

It wasn't yet ten o'clock when her car pulled to a stop near her tent. She jumped out and hurried to the picnic table. There was nothing on it except scars and stains from many years of use. Both attached benches were empty as well.

Discouraged, she sat on the edge of the nearest bench with her elbows on her knees and her hands pressed into her cheeks. It had sounded too good to be true, to return here and magically find her art materials.

She shut her eyes, then opened them and gazed around the campsite. Hopeless. In fact, everything felt hopeless at the moment. Perhaps she had been mistaken about grad school. Was that her destiny after all? Was she just afraid to go that route? The unrest in her heart challenged that idea, but she wouldn't have lost her new watercolour kit if art were her real purpose. She had allowed the words of the man in the park to give her false hope. It was what she had wanted to hear, so it was her own fault.

Annabel stood and turned back toward the car. She dug both hands deep into her pockets, head down, dejected.

As she stepped forward, her left foot hit against something in the short bushes near the table. She bent down to look under the leaves and branches to determine whether she had kicked a stone. Instead she found the bag that held her new art materials lying under the dusty foliage.

"What in the world!" she exclaimed. "How did it get there?"

She retrieved the treasure from its hiding place and dusted off the sides. Thankfulness swelled her heart as she hugged the kit to her chest and hurried back to the vehicle. There was still time to create some art today.

As she drove, she reflected on the conversation she'd had with the gentleman in the park. Again, she wondered how he had known her name. An angel? For a second time, she had no answer.

FIFTEEN

The parking lot at the gardens was now full. Annabel drove around several times and then exited. She turned right and proceeded south along the road until she saw the sign for the hot springs. At the last minute, she changed her mind, drove past the sign, and turned her car back in the direction she had come. She didn't feel like sketching people at the pool.

Before discouragement could enter, she returned to the gardens. Two cars exited just as she drove in. The day wouldn't be a waste after all.

Other tourists now occupied the wooden benches. Annabel walked Muffin through the gardens and found fresh inspiration in the beautiful flowers. She located a vacant area on the grass in full sun. Today was cooler, so the warmth would make things more comfortable for both of them. She spread out the fleece blanket.

Muffin was tired from the walk and turned in a circle several times before settling down. Annabel fed her some treats and then let her alone to rest. She took out the painting kit and set the water dish and paints on the lawn beside her. With her legs bent and crossed, she set the sketchbook in her lap. Flowers needed more detail than a landscape, so she began with a careful drawing.

One thing she recalled was that uneven numbers made a better composition. She arranged the petals, stems, and leaves of three different blooms onto the page with sensitivity. Once more Annabel became engrossed in the pure pleasure of mixing tints and shades of various colours. The multiple layers of glazes created a kind of delicacy the floral painting needed. She continued to shift her eyes from the flowers to the paper as she transformed the formerly blank page into a work of beauty.

The sun warmed her back and shoulders the way the caress of friend's gentle hand would. It added a sense of natural comfort. When she took a break to analyze her progress, she was amazed at the quality of her work. She gave her dog a welcome drink of water, then stretched out her legs, leaned on both hands, and let her head drop backward. Her golden hair touched the blanket behind her.

Suddenly, a bubble of laughter arose within her. She let it escape from her open mouth. The sound floated through the air as a salute to this day, a second day of triumph. A gesture of praise to her God.

Annabel didn't paint through the afternoon. She rested. A lot could be said for simple rest and how it calms the soul. The park was a very pleasant refuge from the troubles she had encountered. She took short walks with her dog and found new places to sit in quietude and solitude. Surrounded by greenery and colour on all sides, she felt satisfied somewhere deep inside. She had her painting. She had been an artist this day.

She settled again on a bench with Muffin. Annabel decided that she didn't just like this place; she loved it. And when the shadows lengthened across the plush lawns and trees stretched their shadows across the flowerbeds, she led her dog to the north side of the park. It was the one area they hadn't yet visited. They descended a shallow flight of stone steps, and then she turned to look back. What a beautiful vista.

Glancing up at the sun's location, she figured she had time for one more painting. She couldn't leave this place without an attempt to paint this view. There would be no time for vacations once she started grad school next month. It might be a long while before she could return, and by then the inspiration would be lost.

Once the blanket was on the ground, she sat cross-legged and began to sketch the scene in graphite. It went surprisingly quickly and easily. Before long, she had effortlessly layered on the colours, connecting with knowledge and skill that had long lain dormant within her. She was more experimental with the hues and let them mingle together wet-in-wet to create the foliage. The effect was luminous.

Just as she put the finishing touches on the painting, she heard a woman's voice behind her.

"How beautiful!"

Annabel lay the brush down and turned to see who had spoken. It was an attractive middle-aged woman whose hands were clasped together in delight.

"Thank you," said Annabel. "That's very kind."

"I really mean it. I have the perfect spot in my house for that beautiful piece. Is it for sale?"

Annabel paused and stared at the woman now extending a hand toward her. She couldn't reply or move. She shook herself out of this momentary shock and reached her own hand to squeeze the woman's fingers gently.

"I'm Anne," the woman continued. "I'm on holiday here in the Rockies from the east. I live near Toronto."

"I'm Annabel."

"What a lovely name. My name is just plain old Anne. Nothing special." She laughed as she ran her hand over the beautiful choker necklace on her long neck.

Annabel nodded and thanked Anne.

"I'm always on the lookout for quality artwork. I haven't found anything here in the shops or galleries that suits me, but your painting is exquisite. The colours and technique are superb. It's full of feeling, and I… well, I just love the scene."

"Yes, it's a lovely place, isn't it? To be honest, I hadn't thought about selling the painting."

The older woman looked disappointed. "Do you have other paintings you would be willing to sell?"

Annabel was overcome with emotion. Although it was her dream to sell her work, she certainly had not expected it to happen on this day. She feared that she might humiliate herself and cry right in front of this stranger.

"I only have a few sketches and one other painting." The watercolour was now dry, so it was safe to flip the pages in her sketchbook. She turned to the scene at the lake.

"Oh my goodness, I would buy that one as well. In fact, I would take either or both of them if they're for sale. Name your price."

There was a hint of pleading in the woman's voice.

Annabel thought a moment. She felt thrilled that someone wanted to buy her paintings yet very reluctant to part with her work.

"If we could exchange contact information…" Annabel began.

"That's an excellent idea."

Anne took a pad of paper and pen out of the little black purse that was slung over her shoulder. She scribbled down some information, ripped the sheet from the pad, and waved it in the air.

"This is where I'm staying in town. The Banff Springs Hotel. And I'm giving you my home contact information as well. Feel free to call collect."

She handed the paper to Annabel, who was still looking up at her.

"Oh, here's some paper," Anne added. "Would you please write down your information?"

Quickly, she wrote her name and telephone number and handed the pad back to Anne.

"I do wish you would sell me one of those paintings today," Anne said with longing.

Annabel smiled. She was about to tell the woman that she hadn't painted in years so she wasn't quite ready to part with her work. But a note of caution in her heart advised her not to do it. Instead she gave a wide, genuine smile and thanked Anne again.

"Keep in touch about the paintings, please," Anne said. "I'm hoping to hear from you before one of us leaves Banff."

"Thank you. I so much appreciate your kind words."

Anne smiled and nodded. She then waved as she strolled away.

Annabel felt on top of the world. She wanted to head to a phone immediately to tell Conner about her painting and the woman who wanted to purchase it. But she had to pack away her things first.

She turned back to the page with the most recent painting. Yes, she was pleased with it. Very pleased with it. She closed the book with a sigh, wondering how much the woman would pay for her work. It wasn't something she had yet considered. It was too early on her journey back to her artist self.

Sixteen

It was early evening when Annabel pulled into her campsite. People all around were busy cooking or already seated at their picnic tables enjoying their meals. The delicious aromas filled the air and Annabel's stomach rumbled with hunger. Food hadn't been a high priority on this trip, but tonight she wanted a proper dinner. She left Muffin in the car while she made her way to the washhouse to boil water.

She rounded the corner of the building on her way back and ran into Benjamin coming from the men's side of the facility. He had obviously just had a shower. His blonde hair was slicked back from his pleasant face. There was a wet towel around his shoulders and a toiletries bag in his right hand. He was whistling as he walked.

"Annabel!" he said with pleasure. "I didn't realize you were in the same loop as me. I haven't seen you around. You must be keeping busy."

"Hi Benjamin. I've been trying to make the most of my short time here." She lowered the volume of her voice with noticeable concern. "How are you doing?"

"I'm okay. This mountain air has a way of smoothing the wrinkles inside one's heart, doesn't it?" He laughed lightly.

"That it does."

"I was hiking today. Tiring, but the exertion, too, makes one feel better."

"Where were you hiking?"

"Up near Johnston's Canyon. Beautiful country. Next on my wish list is a mountain climb."

"That sounds wonderful!" she exclaimed. "It's something I have always wanted to do. Well, Muffin won't be happy if I make her wait much longer for her dinner."

She raised the kettle and gave it a slight shake. Benjamin raised his eyebrows and looked at the kettle.

"She likes it to be warmed first," she added.

They both laughed.

"Some might say she's a little spoiled, but as a vet I understand completely," he told her. "It was nice to see you again. Enjoy your evening, Annabel."

"You, too."

He gave a slight wave, then continued to whistle as he walked away. She was tempted to invite him to join her but decided a quiet evening would be best. There would be time to get the cot ready before dark.

She wanted to call Conner and then have a peaceful evening. It would be the first time she'd really had the chance to enjoy her site since her arrival.

Deep in thought, Annabel mixed the hot water with the dog food in Muffin's bowl and stirred it. She got her dog from the car and put her beside the bowl on the picnic bench. Then she sat and stroked her dog's head as she ate. When the bowl was empty, they walked to the public tap with safe drinking water to rinse it before she went to call Conner. She decided to leave Muffin in the car.

She leaned against the phone booth wall as she dialled her number and went through the regular routine with the automated operator. She tapped her fingers against her thigh as she waited.

She heard Conner answer: "Yes, I will accept the call."

"Conner. It's me."

"I gathered that." He chuckled. "How are you doing today? I more than half-expected you to come home."

His remark rankled. Annabel sighed but kept her voice even. "I'm doing okay. Muffin is great." She knew that would be his next question.

"Good. What have you two been doing?"

"Well, she's with me basically every single second, which is great. Conner, I was painting again today. I found this beautiful garden behind the Parks Canada building, and we spent the day there. We took walks. Ate snacks. And while Muffin slept in the sun, I painted."

It all came out in a rush.

"That's good, sunshine. I'm glad you have this opportunity before grad school to unwind a bit. I can't say that I haven't been worried about you, but it sounds like you're having a nice time after all."

"Guess what?"

"What?" He had a hint of curiosity in his voice.

"A lady offered to buy one or two of my paintings." Her voice carried the pride she felt in this accomplishment.

"Really? Did you sell them?"

"No." She paused, uncertain how to explain. "I decided that I should keep these ones, since I haven't painted in a while. The lady—her name is Anne—gave me her contact information and said to keep in touch. She's interested in getting one of my paintings. I could still sell one or two to her before I leave. She told me where she's staying and invited me to call her there."

"I would like to see them rather than just have you sell them."

"Really?"

"Of course. We could use more art on our own walls. That's what makes your hobby special. You can decorate our home with it." Conner sniffed, then laughed.

"I see," she replied coldly.

Conner picked up on the change in her tone right away. "I'm proud of your talent, Annabel, and I'm glad you're using it. But you have other gifts, too, you know. You're really good with people."

"I'm not certain about that, Conner." She didn't elaborate, and he didn't pursue the subject.

"By the way, I didn't know that you brought paints," he said.

"I didn't. A store here had a watercolour set for a really good price. Half-price." She emphasized this last part. "I felt like painting, and watercolour is the easiest. There's less setup and no need for an easel."

"You have a lot of art materials here."

"Yes, I know, but there wasn't time to find the paints."

"There would have been if you hadn't rushed off."

The old irritation began to rise in Annabel's emotional centre. Conner had never supported her desire to be an artist. He likely never would. He still seemed full of criticism for anything she did, or even the things she didn't do. She had to close the conversation before it derailed her evening.

"Well, I haven't eaten yet, so I better sign off," she said, trying to keep her voice level.

"Look, I'm glad you're enjoying yourself." Conner tried to switch emotional gears and ignored the fact that she hadn't responded to his comment.

"Yes, well… I'll call again. Get a good sleep, okay?"

"Thanks, sunshine."

There was regret in Conner's voice. He hoped and prayed that things would resolve between them and that distance would make her heart grow fonder toward him. Yet he also realized that he seemed to be saying the wrong things. It appeared to be a rut he couldn't get out of for some reason.

"I love you, sunshine."

"Thanks, Conner," she said as she hung up.

Annabel was glad she had left her dog in the car. She set out to walk the loop around the camping area to cool her emotions. She felt let down by Conner. Her enthusiasm for creating art hadn't seemed to rub off on him at all. As far as he was concerned, she would head to grad school in the fall to study counselling psychology. She wasn't at all certain it was the right direction for her to go. Yet she saw his point. After all, what had she done with her art all these years? He would likely wonder whether she was using art as an excuse not to get a proper career.

Benjamin was at his picnic table setting up a small propane stove. A large cooler rested on the table beside him. He looked up as she approached and pointed at the stove. He waved her to come closer.

"You're welcome to join me for dinner tonight. Not that I'm a good cook, but your company would be appreciated. That goes for Muffin, too." He tipped his head and looked up at her as he waited for her reply.

She laughed and put her hands into her back pockets. He was saying all the right things in the right tone. The idea of spending the evening visiting with him appealed to her—that is, until she caught sight of Jan's tent in her peripheral vision.

Benjamin seemed nice enough, but they had just met. She knew very little about him. She felt she was a long way from being emotionally strong, especially after the hurtful conversation with Conner. It was better to be alone.

"It sounds nice, but it's been a long day and I want to get to bed early. Some other time perhaps, if we're both still here."

Benjamin tilted his head and clucked his tongue. "Too bad you'll miss out on my bad cooking. I hope to see you around then."

Annabel nodded. He was charming, and that could spell trouble for her in her present mood. She walked slowly the rest of the way around the loop. At her site, she looked inside the cooler and decided on vegetable soup and a sandwich for dinner. Something hot and something cold. It would make eating an easy chore with little cleanup.

As she moved toward the picnic table, she saw that someone had thrown an orange pop container under the campstove on the far side of her tent. After she ate, she would put it in the bear-proof garbage container down the road.

Dusk was settling like gauze fabric over the mountain. Annabel covered her mouth with her hand as she yawned. The campground had grown quiet as people went off to their evening activities. She was ready for bed, and tonight she would sleep in the tent.

With her sleeping bag, pillows, and blanket over her arm, she unzipped the tent. Cautiously, she stepped inside and looked around. Momentary sadness filled her heart. This was supposed to be her sanctuary for the trip. Perhaps tonight it would be.

She placed a blanket over the cot and carefully rolled out the navy blue sleeping bag. Once the pillows were in place, she laid the woollen blanket on top of the other bedding. She then stepped out of the tent and got her Bible, journal, sleeping clothes, and dog from the car.

Going purely on intuition, she decided to move the car closer to the tent first. Just in case. There was no one at Jan's site, but she did it anyway.

She deposited everything back in the car and moved it parallel to the picnic table and much closer to the tent. Then she gathered her things and entered the tent again, zipping it shut behind her. Her plan was to read a while and then remove the pop container before she fell asleep.

Annabel changed into sweats and a thick hooded sweatshirt. She put her car key around the pointer finger of her right hand so she would know where it was.

Muffin had settled herself at the foot of the cot and Annabel covered her with the blanket. She opened her Bible to the Psalms and began to flip through the pages. The quietness of the evening worked through her like a relaxing massage. Before she knew it, she drifted to sleep.

Seventeen

A sharp call pierced the night and Annabel awoke with a start. She sat upright and listened. The call came again, eerie in the lonely darkness. She stiffened, shivered in the cold, and drew the covers over her shoulders. For a few minutes longer, she waited for more noise but didn't hear anything. She lay back down and turned onto her side, careful not to awaken her dog.

"Go back to sleep!" she told herself sternly, trying to be brave.

Sleep would not return. Annabel turned onto her back and stared up at the ceiling of the tent. She swallowed the huge lump that had formed in her throat and waited. What she waited for, she didn't know.

Then she heard a noise different from the call in the night. Something was moving through the brush to her left.

Her eyes opened wide. Fear arose within and clouded her ability to think. She froze. Turning her head, she saw on the wall an indistinct bulky shadow as something or someone passed close to the tent. She heard a shuffling noise and then a low grunt.

It took a few minutes before she realized what it was. Fear rose to the height of panic as she realized there was a bear outside the thin walls of her tent. Her brain scrambled to create a plan of escape. If she could do nothing else, she would get Muffin to safety. If anything happened to Annabel, Muffin could run off, get lost on the mountain, or worse. She loved her dog too much to let anything happen to her. Someone would find Muffin in the car and let Conner know what had happened.

Annabel stumbled to her feet, shaking like a leaf. She grabbed her dog, her Bible, and her journal. As she approached the zippered door, though, she fell and barely hung on to Muffin. Terror hadn't only made her hands shaky; her fingers had swelled as well. She tried to get the key ring off her finger, but it was stuck onto the thickened flesh.

She put Muffin on the tent floor then turned the key ring around and around, trying to pry it off. Muffin began to growl in a low voice.

"Shhhh!" Annabel pleaded. "Quiet, little girl."

Muffin growled again, just as Annabel pulled the key ring off her finger. It took several attempts to get the zippers undone, first the screen door and then the outer one. She told herself to make a run for the car and not look around at all. At least the car was closer now that she'd moved it.

She made it to the driver's side door and then committed the mistake of looking to the left.

"Oh my…" Her voice trailed off.

There was a cinnamon-coloured bear with its nose at the campstove, trying to get the pop container. The size of it made her feel sick. In an instant, she remembered again that Conner had said that bears could smell something from five miles away. It might have come from very far away to find her here!

Horror filled her heart and her mind; her whole body shook with it. She shoved the key into the lock and turned it. Then she threw Muffin onto the seat. The dog scrambled to the passenger side and growled again.

The bear had noticed her and looked her way. It was exactly what she had hoped to avoid.

Again, Annabel froze as she stared at the beast. Then something inside her released and she heaved herself into the car, slamming the door shut. She pressed the lock button.

With her hands gripping the wheel to steady herself, she wondered what to do next. Would the bear come for the car?

"Lord!" she screamed inwardly with her eyes shut tight. "Lord!"

It seemed an eternity before she opened her eyes again. She glanced over to the stove. The bear was no longer there, but she could make out the remains of a shredded cup on the ground. That could have been her. It could have been her precious Muffin. Why hadn't she thrown that stupid cup away earlier? Who had been so ignorant as to put it there in the first place? Annabel was totally undone.

She grabbed her journal and held it in both hands. If she wrote, perhaps she could calm down. Muffin sat nearby, watching with her soft brown eyes.

Annabel crawled to the passenger seat and gathered her dog into her arms. She was too overwhelmed even to cry.

For the next hour, she rocked her dog and herself as she wrote out the incident. She hadn't written much while she'd been away, but now she transcribed everything she could remember about the trip, and as she did so she grew calmer.

Then she got angry. She was mad that her trip had gone awry. She felt let down. This trip had gone from good to bad to downright ugly. The joy of painting now seemed a flimsy memory. She wasn't just fragile; she was indignant.

Annabel knew what she had to do. If she didn't return to the tent, she would never go into one again. She grabbed her jacket from the back seat, wrapped it around Muffin, and kissed her.

"You'll be safe in here, my girl," she said with more confidence than she felt.

She took the key, locked the car door, and headed back to the tent with all the courage she could muster. First, she sat on the edge of the cot and pulled the hood of her sweatshirt over her head. It hung over her forehead like a protective shield for her mind.

Until dawn, she lay on the cot like a frozen statue. Her eyes didn't close except to blink. She stared straight ahead at the wall in front of her and wondered how things had gotten so out of control. Why had she insisted on coming here? In her mind, she replayed the lyrics of Celine Dion's new song, "All by Myself." That was her reality here; she really was all by herself. She felt the impact of that truth.

When she knew it was light enough outside to see, she forced herself to get up, unzip the tent, and step outside. This seemed like a triumph, even though it had been dangerous to return to the tent with a bear in the area.

She stretched and looked around. It came upon her unsuspectingly, but she realized how weary she felt. The excitement of painting had been an adrenaline boost, but now she felt the weight of exhaustion from another traumatic experience. Restlessness was its companion, and she didn't enjoy the company of either of them. She no longer felt any inspiration.

Annabel reflected on the merits of returning home. Perhaps it would be better to quit while she was ahead and spend the rest of the summer sketching in the city. Although it would make her feel like a flake that she had booked more days only to cancel, she could still ask for a refund. She would call Conner and admit defeat. He would undoubtedly be happy about it.

She sat at the picnic table and ran her hand through her tangled hair. It wouldn't take long to dismantle the tent, and she could be on her way home. She considered her options and wondered whether she would completely lose her motivation for art if she gave up now. There were lots of other places in the mountains she could stay. She could drive further on to Radium Hot Springs. There were a few nice campgrounds there that might be more family-friendly and safe. It didn't have to be here that she spent the rest of her vacation, even though she had always loved this mountain town.

It might be that she was giving up too soon, but her mind was made up. She gathered her long hair and twisted and tucked it into a messy bun with a scrunchy before she set out.

There was a long line of cars waiting along the road to the camp office when she walked there to check out. That looked promising. With so many hopeful campers who wanted spots midweek, she might easily get out of her commitment. It strengthened her resolve to leave.

There was no line of cars waiting to check out, so she walked to the window and was disappointed to see a sign that read "Back in 30 minutes." She looked up toward heaven and sighed heavily.

On her way back to her site, she noticed again the battered cooler with the bear warning sign. It sent a new kind of shiver down her spine. She shuddered and walked more quickly.

As Annabel turned into her camping loop, she saw her green dome tent curved upward amidst the shadows of the morning light. Indifferent, she glanced over at Jan's site. His tent was still there as well, along with an even taller pile of beer and pop cans. Thankfully, there was no sign of him.

She was still looking at his site as she approached her car. She stopped when she heard a voice.

"Where do you go so early every morning?"

It was Jan. He was sitting atop the picnic table beside her tent with his feet firmly planted on the bench.

Annoyed, she glared at him but said nothing.

"Did you know that you wake up half the people here slamming your car door?" he said a bit louder.

"I'm not deaf," she retorted.

"Not a morning person after all, I see." His voice had softened into a teasing tone.

"What are you doing here?"

He smiled. "Obviously, waiting for you. I was disappointed that you leave every morning before I get up, but I knew I would eventually see you because the tent I helped you set up is still here."

"As I recall, I set up my own tent. You broke the pegs."

"Ah, the damsel in distress doesn't appreciate her rescuer."

"Well, I hope you came by to say goodbye, because I'm leaving. And I won't need help taking down my tent."

His eyes widened slightly. He was clearly surprised.

"Why would you leave?" He rose from the table and took a step toward her.

She put her hand up to signal for him to stop. "My business, not yours."

"Look, I'm sorry for being out of line the other night. I was hoping we could still be friends. You could give me another chance. Why don't you take a drive and think it through?"

"I don't need to think it through. I'm on my way home. If you would excuse me, please, I need to get ready."

Annabel moved toward her car. She needed to wash up and feed her dog before she went to check out. This guy didn't have a clue. She had been through enough for one trip, but that, too, was none of his business.

Jan stood up without a word and crossed the road. She looked up to see what he was doing and saw that he had stopped at the edge of his site, his face turned toward her. He did look remorseful. At this point, she didn't care. She needed to take care of her own affairs.

Half an hour later, Annabel was ready to go back to the office to check out. This time, she decided to drive. As she backed slowly down the sloped driveway, she heard a knock on the passenger window.

It was Jan. What now?

She rolled down her window and put her head partway out. "What is it that you want?" she called impatiently.

"I wondered if you could give me a ride to the office. There's a bus that goes into town. I'll miss it if I walk."

Jan had a backpack slung over his shoulder. He looked sincere. She unbuckled her seatbelt and leaned over to unlock the door. Muffin moved onto her lap as she straightened up.

"I can't believe you have the nerve to ask for a ride, and I can't believe that I'm actually going to give you one."

"I'm a person in need and you are a nice person. I helped you. Now you're helping me. Simple." He turned to her and smiled. His intense blue eyes held a sparkle.

They drove in silence toward the office. Annabel pulled over to the side of the road to let Jan out before they arrived. When he didn't move or reach for the door handle, she wondered if there even was a bus into town.

"Look, I'm actually on my way to do a hike," he said. "You said you wanted to climb a mountain. I'm a guide. I can help you achieve that dream. It would only take part of the day. Then you could decide whether or not to leave."

Had she really told him about her personal goal? Her desire to climb a mountain had been a longtime dream. The thought of having shared the information with him was repugnant.

"You won't be able to get your money back if you check out," he continued.

"There's a line of cars waiting to check in."

"That doesn't guarantee it. Come on. One climb. One mountain. Fulfill your dream with someone who knows how to do it. Then leave if you want."

His words echoed in her mind.

Annabel was worn out. She'd not only had a terrifying experience but little sleep. It made her feel more vulnerable. Despite her determination to return to the tent last night, she didn't consider herself a naturally courageous person.

Unbidden, a thought came to her mind. It sounded plausible. She could fulfill her dream and climb a mountain. She knew she could never do it by herself, and now she wouldn't have to try it alone. It would just be a few hours during the day with other people around. Afterward she could get away without compromise.

Jan reached for the door handle and opened the door. He understood that her failure to reply was a certain no. He stepped onto the side of the road and closed the door, then took a few steps straight ahead.

But he paused.

Under the stress of her circumstances, she forgot that the Bible said to test all things—and that included thoughts. Her resolve began to weaken as her heart cried out conflicting messages. A quiet voice encouraged her to phone Conner. A louder one told her to climb a mountain and fulfill a dream.

The light filtering through the trees caught the highlights in Jan's hair and made it shine like gold. There was nothing sinister about him this morning.

Confusion clouded her good judgment and the louder voice in her heart won. She got out of the car just as Jan took a small step back toward the vehicle.

She tried to think rationally about it, but her mind wouldn't go there. She pursed her lips and then bit the lower one. Go or stay? Phone Conner? Climb a mountain? Confusion filled her with indecision.

Finally, she spoke. "Well, if I climb a mountain today, it will be with my dog. If she can't do it, I won't."

"I will personally carry the dog myself."

Annabel glanced at the car where Muffin sat waiting. She hoped she was doing the right thing. She didn't want to do anything more to put them in harm's way.

Jan glanced at his watch. "It's too late to check out today. You're making a good choice. But you'll have to drive. As you know, I don't have a car here," he said, as though it was decided. "Now you will climb a mountain before you go back to the city."

He gently pressed the point because he realized Annabel was still trying to resist. The louder voice in her head gave credence to his suggestions—and she gave in.

Muffin barked from the front seat of the car, but Annabel didn't see a way of escape. She resigned herself to the power of Jan's words. She also didn't recognize the meandering fickleness of her resolve to flee to safety.

"Okay, get in." She heard herself say the words as from a distance.

Muffin moved to the backseat and into her carrier as Annabel slid behind the wheel.

Jan folded his height into the low ceiling of the vehicle. "Small car."

"Do you want to walk?" she asked sternly.

"Very nice car."

Annabel gave a soft grunt as she continued toward the camp office. As she slowed to pass it, she almost stopped to try to check out. Jan noticed and began to talk about his first experience climbing a mountain. The distraction worked. She continued along the winding road that led to the main road and down the mountain.

She pondered the morning as she drove. After her failed attempt to check out and the encounter with Jan, she had washed up, brushed her teeth and hair, and changed into clean clothing in the washhouse. Her face looked ashen in the mirror, but with a bit of makeup on she no longer looked as pale. The purple shadows under her eyes were almost hidden. She had been ready to face the day and move on from this place.

Now here she was driving with the one person she most wanted desperately to avoid. The seducing thoughts that joined with Jan's insistence had won. It was strange that she no longer really sensed the danger she had associated with him. Today, she would fulfill a dream and climb a mountain. She would keep her focus on that fact. Perhaps it would change her life. Annabel convinced herself that it would not only be okay but that it was worth the attempt.

The tugging of her heart to call Conner grew fainter as she pictured the climb in her imagination. In fact, she was no longer listening to her heart at all. She didn't bother to consider whether he would mind that she would spend the day hiking with the same stranger with whom she had dined. If she had given him a chance, Conner might have put on the brakes for her and insisted that she leave.

A seed of rebellion planted in their long-distance communications sprouted at that moment as she remembered their last conversation and his lack of support for what was important to her. She raised her chin in defiance.

Yes, today she would climb a mountain. It was something she wanted, and she didn't need his approval.

EIGHTEEN

Jan gave the directions to Sulphur Mountain, the location of the hike. Annabel drove through town along Banff Avenue and across the bridge before she headed up a steeper slope. She caught a glimpse of the park where she'd painted the day before and briefly thought of that lovely day. The sun had brushed away the coolness of the morning. It was going to be a hot day.

"Do you have snacks and water?" he asked.

She glanced over at him irritably. Her mood had not improved. "I can find something. Do you?"

He patted his backpack and grinned. "I'm always prepared for everything."

"I'll bet you are," she replied in a sarcastic voice.

He wanted to make a suggestive comment, but he stopped himself. Instead he kept the conversation light, otherwise she might turn the car around and kick him out. He didn't want to lose this opportunity to be with her; it was likely his last chance. There was something more he wanted and this time he would be patient.

"I've climbed many mountains," he said. "You have to pace yourself."

"Well, my pace will not be quick, so you may have to go off on your own if you want a faster climb."

"No, I'll stay with you. I don't mind. Have you really never climbed a mountain?"

"I've wanted to but never had the opportunity. In fact, I tried many times to get into the Blue Mountain climbing course, but it was always full."

"What's Blue Mountain?"

"It's an outdoor program north of here near Jasper. They do all kinds of guided nature activities. Mountain climbing is just one. You have to apply by mail on a certain date. They open the mail in the order it arrives and only take the requisite number for each course. My application never got me in."

"Hmm," he said thoughtfully, turning to study her face.

"I even bought expensive hiking boots and broke them in, hoping I would be accepted, but I never was. I didn't bring them because it certainly wasn't my plan to do any climbing on this trip."

"What will you wear?"

"Running shoes."

"I guess that will have to do." He shook his head in mock disgust. He had on his well-worn hiking boots. "Turn left here," he shouted just before they sailed past the turnoff for the Banff Hot Springs.

She slammed on the brakes and barely made the turn.

"Thanks for the advance warning," she said sharply. "Why are we going up the road to the hot springs?"

"Keep going. You'll see."

They drove up the steep road as the sun climbed higher and the car grew warm. Annabel rolled down the window.

"Don't you have air conditioning?"

"If you want air conditioning, roll down your window," she said with a warning glance.

Jan rolled down the window. The cross breeze cooled the car to a reasonable temperature.

They drove along in silence. Annabel was glad not to have to make conversation for the time being.

"Okay, turn left here," Jan said with growing excitement.

"But it's the gondola parking lot."

"Yes. That's where we're going. We climb up and get a free ride down." He sounded nonchalant.

"I don't like heights. Why can't we climb down?"

"It will take too long. There won't be time."

Annabel pulled into one of the few available spots and parked. She stepped out of the car and grabbed her pink backpack. Deftly, she removed all the art materials before she added snacks and her dog's treats and bowl along with several bottles of cold water from the cooler.

They walked together across the crowded lot to a sign that indicated the start of the trail. Annabel looked up. It was a steep incline. Doubts crowded in. What was she doing here? Why hadn't she followed through and left as she had planned? She swallowed uneasily and looked up at him.

"Come on," he said. "You can do it."

They started up the path in silence. Muffin began to tire within minutes. She started to pant, so Annabel picked her up and put her backward over her shoulder. The dog's head bobbed up and down as they continued onward. With the added weight, the effort of the climb quickly began to wear on Annabel.

"Um. Maybe this wasn't such a great idea," she said through laboured breaths.

"Here, I'll take her for a while."

Jan reached for the dog. With a sense of uncertainty, Annabel handed her precious Muffin to the tall blonde man.

"Be careful."

"I will," he said as he dipped the dog over the side of a shallow cliff.

Annabel screamed and instinctively reached for her dog. Jan laughed as he placed the long-haired pup over his shoulder.

They continued without conversation up the steep switchbacks. After the first half-hour, Annabel wondered why she had thought mountain-climbing would be so great. Perhaps she had just been in love with the idea of it. Climbing didn't seem mystical now; it was just a lot of hard work. Her lungs hurt. Her calves were beginning to ache.

"Hey," she said. "I have to stop for a bit."

Annabel's face was red and she was breathing hard. She stopped in the middle of the path and bent down. With her hands on her knees, she rested a moment.

"Okay. No problem." Jan handed back Muffin. "Here's your dog."

She put the puppy on the ground, the leash firmly around her wrist. Then she sat on a smooth boulder at the edge of the path and struggled out of the pack on her back. She placed it on the ground and withdrew the water dish. Muffin lapped at the water until it was empty, then climbed onto her owner's lap. The dog had a lot of heart, but she would likely have to be carried the rest of the way.

Annabel stalled for time. She lifted her chin and tried to peer over the tops of the trees of the dense forest covering the mountain.

"How much further?" she asked.

Jan laughed heartily as he took out a bag of trail mix and offered it to her. She took a small handful, popped it into her mouth, and began to chew the nuts, seeds, and dried fruit.

"Come on. We've barely begun."

Annabel groaned. Perspiration beaded her forehead. She lifted the corner of her peach-coloured T-shirt, bent and wiped the moisture from her face. With resignation, she reached into her backpack and withdrew a bottle of water and the bag of dog treats.

She took a swig of water and wiped her mouth with the back of her hand. She then looked down at her green army shorts, glad she had taken the time to wash up and change her clothes. She opened the bag of dog treats and fed them to Muffin one by one.

"Ready to go?" Jan asked.

"Give me another minute or two, please." Annabel said, too tired even to feel irritated.

"I can't carry both of you, you know."

"I didn't ask you to carry me. I asked for a few more minutes to rest."

Jan turned to look at the last switchback they had ascended. An elderly man and his plump wife came up to the turn slowly and waved a greeting as they passed. He wore a Swiss-style hat at a jaunty angle and used a walking stick he swung energetically with each step.

A group of giggling teenage girls followed. They looked at Jan. One of the prettier girls cupped her hands and whispered into her friend's ear. They both laughed and blushed.

"Let's go before it gets too busy." Jan was insistent.

Truthfully, Annabel longed to give up. Even though she wanted desperately to turn back, it was likely too late to do so now. They had climbed too far. If hiking was this hard, rock-climbing must be gruelling.

She ignored Jan, who was staring at her. The thought of going home returned. This had been her chance to climb a mountain, but now it didn't seem worth the effort. In fact, it seemed like a really dumb idea. She ought to have called her husband and headed home. She'd had something to prove to herself, and maybe to him, but now she was too tired even to remember what that was. She struggled within; she couldn't just stay here forever.

With determination, she stood up and took a deep breath. She made what she considered a brave decision. No longer did she focus on Annabel, the vulnerable woman; deep inside she wanted to be Annabel, the strong woman who climbed mountains fearlessly.

She shook her head with new resolve, shrugged her backpack onto her shoulders, picked up her dog, and turned to face him.

"Let's go!"

During the next hour of climbing, they passed Muffin back and forth many times. Jan talked on and on about his life as a guide, bragging of his prowess, entertaining and distracting her with his slick words.

Halfway up, they came to a cabin just north of the trail at the switchback. They stopped and rested, taking in the magnificent view of mountain peaks and the steep descent to the valley below. It was as though they could see forever. Annabel was mesmerized.

Jan moved closer, placed his arm around her shoulders, and gave her a gentle squeeze. "See, I told you this would be a great experience."

For a moment, she almost forgot herself. She wanted to lean her head against him and feel the comfort of his obvious strength. Instead she collected herself and moved away.

But he had felt it, too, and smiled to himself.

By the end of the second hour, Annabel was so fatigued that she could barely keep moving. Again, she asked to stop for a rest. They sat on the ground in front of the cutline. Her eyes traced the line of trees to the bottom of the mountain. They were really high up. She could hardly believe they had traversed all those switchbacks. No wonder she was so tired. It had been a steep climb!

As though he could read her mind, he said it out loud. "You can't believe you've done this, right? Climbed so high. Isn't it great?"

"Yeah!" Annabel nodded her head.

She had almost made it to the top of a mountain. Jan was helping her accomplish this feat, and he seemed proud of her for it. He couldn't be all that bad.

The inner cautions about him were forgotten for the moment, lost in the experience. She no longer focused on that night, his inappropriate behaviour, the handprint on the window, or the nightmare. This slice of time was all there was, and she immersed herself in it. A weary smile spread over her full lips until it exposed her perfect white teeth.

Jan looked at her mouth with longing in his eyes.

"God is wonderfully present in His creation," she said spontaneously.

He gave her a hard stare, then looked away. It was obvious he didn't like her mentioning God. But the thought consumed her. Gladness filled her tired heart. God was here. She was climbing a mountain, fulfilling a dream. There was no room for warnings or danger, only a joy she hadn't felt in a very long time.

"I wish my husband could see this."

"He could have come if he wanted to."

Jan stood up, a towering mountain over the tiny woman and her dog. Annabel was about to reply, but he beat her to it.

"Let's go," he said in a gentler voice. He reached out his hand and pulled her to her feet.

In less than half an hour, they came to the top of the trail. Jan mounted the bank easily and walked on. The incline was too steep for Annabel to navigate by herself, so she stood there with Muffin in her arms and wondered what to do.

It was several minutes before Jan returned. He looked down at her, shook his head, and reached for the sleepy dog. Then he extended his left hand toward her. When their hands connected, she felt a surge of electric spark travel up her arm and land somewhere near her heart. She drew in a sharp breath. The pure physicality of this challenging journey had connected them.

Jan pulled as she pushed her running shoe into the dirt and rocks. Up she went step by step. The final tug almost landed her in his arms.

His eyes were bright and beckoning. If he tried to kiss her now, she knew she wouldn't be able to resist. She forced herself to laugh loudly as she disengaged her small hand from his large warm one.

Two ebony crows flew from a nearby tree with throaty caws, which made her laugh authentically. She reached for her dog and buried her face into the thick hair.

"I simply can't believe it," she said. "I climbed a mountain. I really did."

Annabel was no longer thinking of her husband or home. She was caught up in this moment with a heart that was far too open. The climb had rendered her exhausted and the triumph made her vulnerable in ways she had never before experienced.

Jan watched her face silently, knowing that his goal had been made less difficult. It would be as easy as taking candy from a child.

"Let's get a tea," he suggested, remembering that it was her favourite drink.

There was a structure ahead and they walked around the corner of the building side by side. A barrier along the outside of the path provided safety, but beyond were breathtaking views. They passed the gondola launch. Next, there was a gift shop. Further on was a café.

"Earl Grey, okay?" he asked.

"Yes," she replied with a wide smile. "Thanks. One of my favourites."

"I know."

Annabel waited outside with her dog in her arms. Jan brought out two steaming cups of tea with teabags on top of the lids.

They both leaned against the sturdy stone wall. She put the cup on the ledge, then ripped open the packet. Jan reached for the paper and threw it in a nearby garbage can. She dipped the teabag into the water, fully appreciating the aroma of oil of bergamot. When it was the desired strength, she removed the bag. Jan reached for it and tossed it away as well.

Annabel sipped her tea. The hot brew was exactly what she needed, refreshing despite the heat of the day.

"I'm going up that trail." He motioned to a path that led further north to a more distant location. "Do you want to come?

She looked at the rise and fall of the trail and shook her head. "No. I'm okay here. You go ahead. I want to enjoy my tea."

"You'll be here when I get back?" he asked.

"Yes, of course. Where would I go?"

Annabel watched as he walked away from her, glad for some time alone with her dog. Two people vacated a spot at a nearby table. She sat down after placing her tea on the surface. With her silky blonde hair in a long ponytail and her face flushed from exertion, she looked even more beautiful than usual. Muffin sat on her lap and attracted a lot of attention. People stopped to ask questions, leaned close to greet the dog, or patted her head. Acting the goodwill ambassador as usual, Muffin reacted with pleasure.

Upon his return, Jan watched from afar. He frowned at the people stopping to talk to Annabel. Laughing and chatting, she was creating a stir and receiving a lot of interest.

She glanced up and saw him watching her. He didn't look happy. She wondered what was up.

Slowly, he walked over. "I saw you talking to many people."

"Really? There are a lot of interesting people here. My beautiful girl is the one who gets all the attention, and she deserves it." She stroked Muffin's head.

"You're the one who's beautiful." He let it slip casually, but his eyes were fixed intently on hers.

Annabel felt a slight shiver, but this time she pushed aside the inappropriateness of the comment and laughed. She allowed the whole experience of the mountaintop to warm her. The victory of climbing the mountain had crowned her vacation, despite the challenges it had presented. She would relish every single minute of this.

"If you say so." She flipped her head, making her ponytail dance behind her.

Jan reached out to touch her hair as it swung close, but then he dropped his hand. The temptation of those golden strands would have to wait. He wasn't going to spoil the moment or lose his chance with her.

The banter between them became easy. Annabel was relaxed from the physical output of the climb and felt happier than she'd been in a long time. Jan made himself a perfect companion with his quips about the people walking by them. At times he made comments about women in the hope of making her jealous, but she just giggled. For her, the time with Jan had become a delight. She'd forgotten about time, danger, or leaving for home.

"I hate to say this, but we probably have to go back down," Jan said with reluctance. "It's getting late and the gondola will stop soon enough. Get into line, okay?" He motioned with his head toward the men's room. "I'll be right back."

Annabel looked at the lineup for the gondola. The long, unruly queue followed the curve of the building and she wondered how long it would take to get to the head of it. More seriously, she wondered whether she was brave enough to get into one of those round containers and fly down the mountain in it. She didn't like heights. This was one ride she didn't want to take.

But she got into the queue anyway.

She thought Jan had returned and was beside her, but he wasn't there when she turned to speak to him. She stood on her toes to see over the crowd and spied him walking back toward the trail.

"Hey!" she called. "Over here!"

He stopped and turned. A grimace carved his features into a macabre mask. She motioned with her free hand and he walked toward her with his head down. His hands clutched the straps of his backpack at the top of his shoulders.

"I'm not going on this thing alone, if that's what you thought." She said it softly because she understood in that moment that he was more afraid of heights than her. If she could help him to calm down, she was certain he wouldn't leave her to face the gondola ride alone. It was the best thing for both of them. "Come on. If I can do it, you can, too."

They were at the head of the line now. The man who worked the cars swung the door open and told them gruffly to get in. She stepped inside delicately and sat down with her back to the descending mountain. Jan climbed in half-heartedly and sat opposite her. Two young men pushed their way in and also sat opposite each other, one beside Annabel, the other beside Jan.

When the door slammed shut, the car took off along the cable and catapulted them through the air. Annabel let out a piercing scream that made the two fellows howl with laughter and try to rock the car.

"No!" she shouted.

Jan croaked out a command of his own. "Stop it!"

This made them stop rocking, but more laughter followed. It was a wild ride down, with Muffin shaking in Annabel's lap. She hung onto her dog for dear life.

These moments of torture seemed endless. There was no way to enjoy the view; her eyes were closed and her teeth ground together between squeals of sheer terror until the car finally slowed and arrived at its destination at the bottom.

A young woman with a peaked hat pulled low over her eyes and a jacket two sizes too big grabbed the door and swung it open. Annabel scrambled out first, clutching her dog. The two young men jumped out next, shaking their heads and still chuckling as they walked away.

A clearly shaken Jan emerged last, trying to cover his fear with a feeble smile.

"Let's get out of here!" They said it in perfect tandem.

Joined in their triumph and fear, they made their way to her car with wobbly steps. Soon they were descending the steep hill back to the valley where the town lay in sunshine.

They passed a church along the way with a sign that read "God is talking. Are you listening?" Annabel noticed but turned her eyes back to the road and put it immediately out of mind. Instead she concentrated on the anecdote Jan was telling. He had already recovered from the gondola escapade.

Nineteen

As the vehicle crossed back over the bridge along Banff Avenue, Jan threw his arm outward and pointed left toward the park. Annabel noted to herself that she had begun the day there after her first night here. An uneasy feeling edged its way into her consciousness.

"Let's stop here for a bit," Jan said with enthusiasm.

She pulled into the first available spot, which thankfully was far from where she had been that morning. A cluster of spruce trees gave some shade to the little blue car. Annabel sighed. She hadn't planned to spend the whole day with him.

"Well, here we are," she said, not at all eager to be there.

He pointed to a spot. "Let's get out and sit under the trees in the shade."

"Well, we already have shade," she murmured.

But she reached for her dog and stepped outside. They hadn't eaten in hours except for trail snacks. She was hungry after so much exertion and no lunch. Muffin had only eaten dog treats, so she opened the treat bag and held several out for her dog. Muffin crunched them eagerly and asked for more. Annabel's stomach rumbled, to her embarrassment.

A new awkwardness filled the air. On their long hike, she had let down her guard and begun to feel as though Jan was an old friend. Dismayed, she realized that she had even considered him a potential love interest as they visited atop the mountain. The day had given rise to excitement, but as the sun began its downward journey toward the tops of the trees, her mood likewise joined the descent.

The amphitheatre at the far end of the park was empty. They strolled quietly in that direction.

"Do you want to sit here?" he asked.

"Any place is okay." She hadn't meant to sound curt.

"I didn't know you were moody."

"You don't know me at all, actually, nor I you."

Annabel sat on the steps and placed Muffin beside her. She looked up into his intense blue eyes, which now wore a fierce look.

"What do you expect?" he said. "We only met a few days ago."

"Nothing. I expect nothing."

And she meant it. Her holiday had been jeopardized more than she was willing to admit to herself. She was tired and hungry. In fact, she didn't really want to be here with this man at all. She wasn't a toy and life wasn't a game to trifle with; it was important. She would prefer to be alone with her dog.

Jan picked up on her musings. He had spent a lot of time with many different people. Reading them was easy for him. What he said next would determine the outcome of the evening. He knew he had to be careful, so he softened his tone.

"I'll go to the grocery store and pick up something for dinner," he said. "We can go back to my campsite, and I'll cook."

"Again? That's not fair."

"I enjoy cooking."

He rose before she could reply and loped off with long strides.

Annabel was thankful to have some time alone. She leaned back against the step and closed her eyes. Her mind was blank. Weariness filled her soul, but she didn't think about praying. She just rested in the quiet shade.

She must have drifted off, because she awoke startled and uncertain where she was. The sleepless night was taking its toll.

"You're drooling," Jan said. "Not attractive."

"No, I'm not!" Annabel lifted a delicate hand to her mouth.

There was no drool. He was making a joke, but she didn't find it particularly humorous. She looked at him with a frown before slowly pushing herself to a standing position. With slow, stiff steps she led Muffin back toward the car. Her desire to be a superhero mountain climber had been left behind.

With effort, she bent to climb into the car with aching muscles. If she were on her own, she would have gone to the hot springs to soak off the aches and pains. Instead she headed back to the campsite as the sun sank lower and began to disappear into the treetops.

It was nearly dark when they arrived. She backed into her site and shut the car off.

"Did you want to freshen up?" Jan asked.

Surprised, she turned toward him. She could take it as an insult or politeness. Did she smell from the climb? She decided that it didn't matter. She would take the opportunity to clean up, change, and feed her dog.

"I suppose that's a good idea." Her tone suggested that it was not.

"I'll start to cook," he said quickly as he exited the car. "I'll see you in a while."

He looked down at the plastic bag he held. Then he crossed the road to his site, put the bag on the table, and walked to his tent. He knelt to unzip the door and reached inside to retrieve a plastic bin. His backpack was on the ground beside him. He shoved it into the tent and zippered the door shut.

Annabel stood silently by her car. All she wanted was to lie down on her comfortable cot, be quiet, and rest. She didn't want to expend any more emotional energy visiting. It didn't even occur to her that she had forgotten to phone her husband.

She busied herself preparing the dog food, then sat watching Muffin gobble it down hungrily. Afterward they went to the washhouse, and entered the ladies' side. Annabel put her tote bag on the counter and placed soap and a small towel beside it. She hung a fresh long-sleeved T-shirt, jeans, and undergarments on a wall hook.

"Sit nicely," she crooned to her pup.

Obedient and eager to please, Muffin curled up on the floor beside her. She kept her eyes on her owner. Annabel decided she would wash up at the sink.

A deep female voice spoke to her. "If only we could all be as good as you."

Annabel turned to see who it was. A large woman with a green baseball cap shoved over dark curls stood just inside the door. Annabel nodded silently. The woman turned and entered the shower area. A few moments later, Annabel heard the sound of running water. She wanted to take a shower, too, but felt pressured to return to Jan's site for dinner.

She didn't know why couldn't she just decline. Perhaps she felt indebted because he had helped her climb the mountain. She remembered that her mother had always told her not to feel beholden to anyone. But that's exactly what she had done and now she understood her mother's wisdom.

Annabel looked at herself in the mirror. Her face looked young and vulnerable, more like a child than an adult. She rubbed her cheeks and forehead with ivory soap and then rinsed with warm water. As she patted her face dry, she wondered where all the years had gone. Thirty-nine.

"But still attractive to handsome strangers," she said as she forced a smile.

She continued to look at herself in the long mirror as she removed the peach T-shirt that now had sweat stains under the arms. Quickly, she washed her torso and arms, dried, and put on the clean top. The legs and feet were next, and she concluded her freshening up with clean undergarments and jeans. All the while, she ignored the nagging tightness that had begun to form in the centre of her chest.

A bit of makeup would help her feel more dressed, even though it meant she had to return later to wash it off, which wasn't a pleasant thought. She carefully put on eyeshadow and liner to enhance her expressive green eyes. When she opened her lips slightly to put on a luscious pink lipstick, she paused a moment. Why was she dolling herself up for a meal with someone she didn't want to be with anyway? The climb had been fun, but it was over now.

Stop being so dramatic, she scolded herself. *It's only dinner with a fellow camper who helped me reach my goal of climbing a mountain.*

Everything would be innocent enough. She would make certain of it.

"Remember your promise to be more positive?" she reminded herself. "Bask in the glow of your victory. You'll most likely never climb another mountain."

But Annabel had no smiles left. Feeling tired and down, she gathered her things and stuffed them in her bag.

She and Muffin walked around the campsite loop before returning to the car. The dog slowly investigated the ground and took her time finding the right spots to relieve herself.

When they passed Benjamin's site, Annabel noticed that his rental vehicle was gone. Why that bothered her, she didn't know.

They completed the loop and she put her things into her car.

"Don't bring the dog!" Jan called from across the road. His voice had a hard edge to it. He meant it.

Annabel glanced down at her loving companion's soulful eyes. "Do you want to stay and sleep?"

It sounded like a good idea. It had been a long day for Muffin, and she would benefit from the rest. Annabel rolled all the windows down low enough to keep the car cool and the air fresh.

The evening air was growing crisp, so she grabbed the fleece blanket to cover Muffin. Reluctantly, the dog stepped onto the passenger seat, then jumped to the back seat and slunk into to her carrier. She turned around, lay down, and looked up at Annabel with pleading eyes.

"You'll be okay, little girl. I won't be long. I promise."

The dog sighed and continued to gaze up at her with mournful eyes. Uninvited, tears filled Annabel's eyes, but she locked the car door and pocketed the key.

Within minutes, she was seated again at Jan's picnic table, surrounded by the mountain of empty beer and pop cans. She pulled the sides of her beige cardigan sweater closed and did up the buttons. With her arms folded on the table, she rested her head on them.

"Tired?" Jan asked.

"Yes."

"You could lay down for a bit in my tent if you like."

Annabel raised her head. She wasn't that tired. "I'm fine here."

"I had a great time today." Jan smiled broadly.

"I had a good time, too. Thanks again for helping me reach a lifetime goal." She meant it, but her voice held no enthusiasm.

"Glad to do it."

Jan served camp roasted potatoes and fried sausages onto two blue metal plates. He brought them to her side and placed them on the tablecloth. There was a bowl of mixed greens with a large plastic fork and spoon. A bottle of creamy white salad dressing waited nearby and dinner rolls still in the plastic bag. The same white candle rested on the far side of the table.

Instead of sitting across from her, Jan lowered himself onto the bench beside her and faced away from the table. He stretched his long legs in front of him.

"You don't mind, do you?" he asked. "Me sitting on the same side as you?"

Annabel didn't respond.

He reached over and pulled the candle closer. With one deft movement, he'd pulled a red lighter from his pocket and lit it. It wasn't completely dark yet, but it would be soon. The sky was the light blue-grey colour of watered-down India ink. The stars were barely visible, but they began to etch a pattern of light upon the emerging night sky.

As Jan leaned over, his scent wafted over her. He smelled of the outdoors. Fresh pine needles, cool mountain air, rushing cold water, and something sweet she couldn't identify. The power of it almost made her swoon.

"Ready to eat?" he asked with tenderness.

Jan had chugged several beers while he cooked. Now he uncorked a bottle of sparkling wine, poured it into a plastic glass, and held it out to her. She declined with a slight smile and shake of the head. He reached forward and placed it right in front of her before pouring one for himself.

"Look, I'm not a one-night stand," she said defensively. "I'm someone to fall in love with."

"I don't fall in love, okay? Let's eat."

Neither of them spoke more than a few words as they ate. There didn't seem to be much to say.

Partway through the meal, Jan got the campfire going. The logs hissed into the night like snakes. Sparks danced in the night breeze, adding an intoxicating backdrop to the nearly silent meal.

Jan laid his utensils on his empty plate and turned to face her. “I would play music if I had a way to do it. Or I would sing if I had the voice for it.”

Annabel was staring at the crackling flames, but his low, husky comment made her glance over at him. One corner of her mouth turned up and she shook her head. Her eyebrows came together to create an indent of inquisitive bewilderment.

She covered her mouth as she yawned involuntarily. “What an idea. Why would we need music?”

“Romance, dear Annabel.”

Jan took the fork from her hand and placed it on the table. Before she could protest, he grasped both of her hands and pulled her from the bench. She stumbled, but he held her up and drew her close.

Instantly, she was in his arms. He began to hum into her ear as he held her close. With deliberation, he moved her body in time with his in a slow dance. His feet shifted over the ground in his old hiking boots and made a scraping sound.

As he turned her in circles, it made her feel increasingly dizzy. She could smell the European beer on his breath. At first she tried to resist and even pulled away, but he held her tight in an unwanted embrace.

“What do you think you’re doing?” she sputtered.

“Enjoy the moment.” His mouth grazed her ear as he leaned down to hold her tight.

She was no match for him in size or strength and her heart began to beat fast. He held her against himself so firmly that she could feel the pace of his heart quicken, too, but for a different reason.

And the two became one flesh… The words came to her heart unbidden.

"No," she said with determination. "No!"

Annabel tried to scream, but the words got lost as the logs crackled and sparked. He was clearly past trying to seduce her. Increasingly, there seemed no way out. The melody he hummed seeped into her consciousness. She had been aware of his plan, and it hadn't changed since the day she met him. This realization made her nauseous and unsteady. If he let go, she would drop to the ground.

"Isn't this what you long for?" he said. "Romance? A star-filled night of love? Isn't that why you're here without your husband? You came looking for me and you found me."

He pressed her close, feeling her form against him. He was full of desire and certain she was, too. Jan knew he would reach his goal. Here was one more notch for his belt, and this one would make the best memory he'd ever had. She had been a challenge. Tonight was the night. Nothing would prevent his conquest.

Annabel felt utterly exhausted as panic filled her mind. She did long for romance. She ached for attention, affection, and understanding. But it wasn't from him that she wanted these things. An image of Conner floated across the screen of her mind. She wanted her husband, not this deeply disturbed man. But Conner was so far away and couldn't help. There was no way to reach him.

The combined effects of the starry night and the beautiful woman who belonged to another man but who would soon be his intoxicated Jan more than the alcohol. Holding her close, surrounded by the enthralling aroma of femininity, melting candle wax, and fresh mountain air thrilled him.

Annabel wondered why she had lowered her inhibitions. How she wished she had left Banff and never given him a ride that morning. Now her purity and safety were at stake. She was here with an unstable stranger, a madman. Her calls for help brought no response. She had tried, but there was no way to wrench herself from his grasp.

Jan brought his face close to hers and leaned in. Before she could say a word, his lips landed softly on her mouth. He tried to force his tongue past her lips to explore. He let out a groan of desire. She gagged.

Annabel closed her eyes a moment before she opened them again. She had to fight hard.

Again, she tried to push him away, but he held her even tighter. In that moment, fear burst open inside. Spiritual darkness surrounded her. There really was no way out. She didn't know how much time she had before it was too late. She forced her head away from his face.

"Lord!" she cried as loudly as she could. "Help me, my God! Help me!"

Muffin's bark hit the air squarely, resounding again and again. She pawed at the window. Jan turned to look over at the car as a blow hit his head. It gave Annabel the moment she needed to escape.

"I'm used to dealing with animals!" Benjamin shouted as he threw a punch at Jan's jaw. "But none so vile as you!"

Annabel blinked and saw that the other camper's rental car was parked nearby. The driver's side door hung open. Perhaps he had been returning from dinner in town? In any event, he had arrived just in time.

Benjamin hit Jan again, this time squarely on his face. The taller man staggered but didn't fall. A trickle of blood dripped from the corner of his mouth. Jan licked at it, tasting his own blood before swiping at it with his large hand. He then wiped his hand on his jeans and rushed at Benjamin with both arms up, letting out a feral growl. He grabbed the collar of Benjamin's expensive plaid jacket and tried to wrench him to the ground. Benjamin pushed him back, then grabbed his right arm and twisted it behind him.

"Run, Annabel!" he called. "Run and get out of here. I'll deal with this baboon."

"Baboon!" Jan roared. "I'll show you who's the monkey."

Benjamin tightened his grip as he turned his head to see if she had gotten to safety. "Go!"

Annabel stood in the middle of the road in shock, not moving. Her small hands covered her mouth, her large green eyes stricken.

"Get into your car and lock the doors!" Benjamin cried. "Do it now!"

She backed away to the slope that led into her tent site, then stumbled to her car. Shaking, she unlocked the door and collapsed onto the driver's seat. She pushed the lock button in an instant and leaned her arms and head on the steering wheel.

Jan took the few seconds of distraction to wrench himself away from the other man's grip. He broke away and ran to the edge of his site.

"Annabel!" he shouted. "I do love you!"

Benjamin came from behind and knocked him to the ground. Jan was breathing heavily and didn't rise this time.

When Annabel opened the car door to see what was happening, Muffin leaped out barking and ran across the road. She bit deeply into Jan's ankle. Growling, she bit again, even harder, before running back to Annabel, who scooped her up and put her on the car seat. She scrambled to the passenger side, panting, and raised her paws to the window, barking viciously while standing on her hindlegs.

Annabel needed to get out of this place, away from danger she had played with and never fully understood. Her rebellious attitude had almost cost her everything. All she wanted was to be in her husband's arms again, to hear him tell her all the things that would make her feel safe again. But he might as well have been a million miles away.

She started the engine and drove forward. In her side mirror, she saw Benjamin standing overtop the collapsed figure on the ground. He put his hand on his heart, on his lips, and then waved as she left. He would know what to do. She drove off and didn't look back again. She would never have a chance to thank him.

The moon shone brightly in the dark sky, the stars forming their constellations overhead and creating pinpricks of light in the velvet night. She drove through the darkness toward the light poles at the park office.

She slowed as she came near the exit sign and found the building itself to be dark. Several garbage cans stood on a wooden platform for campers to deposit their refuse. Annabel looked over at them as she proceeded. Someone had left a white trash bag nearby. She shook her head.

"Unbelievable," she whispered.

Surprised, she noticed something move. Out from between the trees, a huge form emerged and lumbered toward the bag. Annabel stopped the car and stared. Through her partially opened window, she heard the unmistakable grunts of a black bear. She watched in horror as the creature grabbed the bag between its enormous paws and then turn a shaggy head toward her. Its beady eyes caught the gleam of her headlights.

The bear lifted its pointed muzzle into the air and let go of the bag, which dropped to the ground with a thud. Shaking its head, the bear opened its mouth wide and roared as it swiped a paw in the air.

Annabel's blood ran cold. Her whole body convulsed as she drove on. A natural marauder. A wild, unpredictable beast.

And yet the human predator she had just encountered was much more dangerous. Tonight had been a narrow escape.

She continued down the road with tears streaming from her eyes. Muffin snuggled close with her head on Annabel's lap. Benjamin and Muffin, her rescuers. God had used them to save her from the consequences of her foolishness and prideful rebellion.

Annabel navigated the curving mountain road cautiously, driving until she found a payphone on the main street and parked right outside it. It was almost midnight and her hands shook uncontrollably as she tried to dial her number.

Finally, she pressed zero and an operator answered. The woman tried hard to convince Annabel to use the automated system before finally understanding that this was an unusual situation. Graciously, she made an exception and put the call through herself.

The phone rang until the answering machine clicked on.

"I'm sorry, miss, but no one is answering. Would you like to try your call again later?"

"He's probably asleep. He will answer. If you could just try again," Annabel pleaded.

Conner picked up on the next attempt. He accepted the collect call with a sleepy voice.

"Annabel? I've been worried about you, sunshine. Why didn't you call?"

She had no answer except the tears that streamed down her lovely face and the giant sobs that made her chest heave.

"Annabel, what's wrong?"

She found her voice long enough to ask him if he could come to Banff the next day. Conner didn't protest. He agreed to take a day off work, rent a car, and come to her. He didn't ask any questions.

"Go to that motel," he suggested. "The one that takes dogs. Don't worry that you don't like it. If they have a room, go for it, okay?" He used his best husband voice to persuade her.

Annabel nodded her head, forgetting that he couldn't see her.

"Understand? I'll come tomorrow and take the tent down. It's okay to be scared. Camping alone when you are a woman doesn't always work out. It's okay."

The comfort of his words washed over her. She didn't deserve his grace and love. He didn't know what she had done.

How foolish she had been about so many things! Annabel put her right hand to her head and rubbed the temple. A major headache was settling in.

"Call me after you check in, okay?" he said. "It will be all right."

Her tears continued to flow. "Okay."

Annabel hung up and returned to her car with her head hanging down. She drove the few blocks to the motel, then parked and entered the motel office with faltering steps. The male clerk looked at her with alarm. Annabel figured she must look in shock. Perhaps he'd even think she needed medical attention.

"Your sign said vacancy." Annabel's voice was shaky.

"I was just about to close the office for the night, but I happen to have one room left. It's yours if you like."

"I have a dog."

"You're in luck. It's a pet room." He handed her a card and a pen.

Annabel filled out the form and signed it. She produced her credit card for the deposit. "I'll be paying cash in the morning."

The clerk nodded as he found the key. "You're lucky to be in a motel tonight, little lady."

The man scratched his head, then grabbed the local newspaper and slid it over to her. The headline read *Missing Female Campers.*

Her eyes slid over the text. A European male pretending to be a camp guide had been implicated in the disappearance of three young women. One had been found stuffed in a food locker on Tunnel Mountain. There was a warrant out for his arrest.

Jan's face swam before Annabel's eyes. She almost fainted.

"They say that guy is still around here, but no one has been able to identify him. He must be hiding out somewhere. He sounds like a really slick character. You're lucky that you'll be safely tucked into a bed in a motel." He handed her the key. "Down the hall to your right. At the end of the hallway, second last room. It's close to a door in case your dog needs to go out. You can park out front in the light. I'll stay open until you get in. Enjoy your stay and get some rest. He lowered his glasses and looked intently at her.

Annabel took the key and turned to leave. Then she looked back. "Thank you."

"That's all right. You just get some rest. It looks like you had a long journey today."

"Yes, you could say that."

She exited the office and moved her car. Thankful for the lights, she grabbed a few items from the car, put Muffin under her arm, and locked the door.

It was easy to find her large and comfortable room. Right away, Annabel called to let Conner know she was safe. Then she took a warm shower, lathered herself again and again, and let the soapy water run into her mouth. She wanted to feel clean.

When she climbed into the cozy bed with Muffin right beside her, she kissed her dog and reached for her Bible. It felt like she hadn't read it in years, even though at home she read it daily. She opened the Holy Book and read:

> No temptation has overtaken you except something common to mankind; and God is faithful, so He will not allow you to be tempted beyond what you are able, but with the temptation will

> provide the way of escape also, so that you will be able to endure it.[4]

Annabel began to sob. She had faced trials and temptations, but God had done what was impossible for her to do. He had provided her with a way of escape. He had been faithful to her.

She hugged her Bible, thanking Him over and over until she finally cried herself to sleep.

---

[4] 1 Corinthians 10:13.

TWENTY

Conner arrived in the early afternoon. He was blessed to secure a rental car first thing in the morning. To get to Annabel as quickly as possible, he pushed the speed limit and didn't stop at all. He sensed that his beautiful wife was in deep trouble. Frankly, he didn't even care what the predicament was—as long as she was safe.

They had agreed to meet outside the motel after he packed up the tent and checked out of the campground.

Conner got the campsite number from the park attendant and let him know that they were checking out. There was no refund offered. Usually he was frugal with finances, but this time he didn't care.

He drove to the tenting area and located their green-domed tent. As he pulled the pegs out one by one, he glanced up at the tall blonde man watching him from across the road, perched atop the picnic table. The site was a mess, empty cans strewn everywhere. Conner felt a spontaneous mistrust of this man. He was glad that Annabel had listened and gone to the motel.

Conner put the cot and bedding in the back seat of the rental. The tent and tarp went into the trunk. He slammed it shut and got behind the wheel.

He heard a hissing sound through the open window. It was the man on the table opening a beer and chugging it down right in the middle of the afternoon. Conner shook his head in disgust and drove off.

He found Annabel sitting on a bench in a patch of shade outside the motel with Muffin on her lap. He walked toward them, then stopped and watched as his wife stroked their dog's head. She looked small and pale, the most vulnerable he had ever seen her.

She looked up when she heard footsteps and noticed him right away. When she smiled weakly and lifted her hand in a wave, he walked toward her with brisk steps. Slowly she stood up with Muffin in her arms. Conner quickened his pace and wrapped them both in a fierce hug. Their little dog, sandwiched between them, began to wriggle and reached her tongue to lick his face.

"Hello, sweetie," Conner crooned to their pet as he stroked her head.

He reached with his other hand and ran it down his wife's blonde curls. Then he kissed the top of her head.

Annabel breathed in his scent. To her, Conner smelled like everything good and clean. She began to cry.

He pulled away from her and held her by the shoulders, gazing lovingly into her eyes. "What is it, sunshine?"

"I love you. I love you so much." The tears flowed heavier as he pulled her close in a tender embrace.

"I love you, too."

Conner waited until the weeping subsided before beckoning for her to sit down. He perched on the edge of the bench beside her. There was business to attend to before they could leave.

"Can you stay here while I see about returning the rental?" he asked. "Or do you want to come with me?"

"I'll wait here for you," she said quietly.

"Have you eaten anything?" He was alarmed at how pale and drawn her face looked. When she shook her head, he added, "Wait here. I'll be right back. Don't talk to anyone, okay?"

She nodded and sat again on the bench with her dog in her arms. There was no expression on her face. She looked blank and haggard.

Conner lost no time. He returned fifteen minutes later with a grocery bag.

"There's cheese and some scones, okay?" He knelt beside her and rubbed her arm.

"I'm not really hungry."

"Ah, but you will eat it for me, won't you, sunshine? I won't be long."

Conner transferred the camping equipment to Annabel's car, having made arrangements to drop off the rental. He found the location easily, paid, and shoved the paperwork into his back pocket before starting back to find his wife. She was still sitting on the bench waiting for him. He would have to drive them home.

As he approached, he called out in a positive voice so as not to startle her. "Hi sunshine. I'm back. Did you want to do anything before we leave? Do you want to show me the park you found? Go shopping? Anything else?"

She shook her head to every suggestion. Conner took Muffin from her and then held her hand as they walked to the car.

"Everything is ready, sunshine. I'll drive if that's okay."

Annabel answered by entering the passenger door and strapping on the seatbelt. Conner drove north along Banff Avenue toward the highway, and soon they were heading toward Canmore. After that, they would leave the mountains behind them.

Annabel fell asleep on the way and he just let her rest. She only awoke as they drove through Calgary, where he picked up some burgers and fries at a drive thru they both enjoyed. Annabel didn't eat much and soon fell asleep again.

When they reached Red Deer, Conner stopped for gas. Annabel got out to walk the dog. After he paid the bill and moved the car away from the pumps, he went out to meet his wife.

"Conner, I need to talk to you." Her voice was barely a whisper.

"Maybe it could wait until we get home?" he suggested pragmatically. He wanted to get back at a decent hour. But in honesty, he was also reticent to hear what she would say. "If we don't leave soon, we'll get home pretty late, sunshine. Are you certain it can't wait?"

"No. I just want to deal with it now, please." She took a deep breath, handed him the dog leash, and turned away. "Please don't be angry, but I don't think I want to go to grad school. I know you want me to, but I don't think it's God's path for me. I think He wants me to be an artist. Just an artist. I'm sorry I haven't done much with my art for a long time. I'm so sorry about so many things."

Conner was silent for what seemed to be an eternity. She braced herself for a sound rebuke. She turned around, but she couldn't look at him.

"Annabel, I was terrified you were going to tell me you were leaving me." He breathed a sigh of relief.

She shook her head and tried to smile.

"Sunshine, I just want you to be safe and happy. I thought grad school was what you wanted. You applied and seemed enthusiastic when you got in. Of course, I was proud of you. It's hard to get into a program like that. God has been speaking to me, sunshine. He and I had a long conversation as I drove up to Banff today. I need to support you in what He wants you to do. In what is meaningful in your life, too. I think I have things to be sorry for as well."

"Oh Conner. What do you have to be sorry about?"

"Making work too important. Worrying so much about finances that I forgot there are more important things. I want time with you and Muffin."

"I want that, too. I just wanted so much to make you proud of me that I looked for some way to go further in my education. I thought you were embarrassed of me. I made a mistake. I did it all without considering whether it was really God's best for me. I've denied the artist in me for a long time, Conner. I've been so miserable for so long."

"The last thing I want is for you to be miserable."

"I want God's best for me. I want to use the gifts He has given me for His purposes and glory. I want what is best for us. Certainly, this will make us both happy. I know that I could change lives with the master's degree in psychology, but I think that I can do that with art, too. I think God wants me to bring beauty and even healing to people through art. I know it's 1996 and we're in an economic recession, but there are more important things than money, right?"

Conner watched her face carefully. He nodded thoughtfully.

"That sounds plausible," he replied. "Well, we can't resolve this whole issue in a gas station parking lot. Can we head for home now?" He held out his hand toward her.

"Okay, but I want to know if you're okay with the artist thing. For me to focus on being a real artist."

"Yes, sunshine. Be what God wants you to be. What He made you to be. We'll pray that God blesses your gifts. You have my full support."

They both smiled as they walked back toward the car.

"Do you want me to drive for a while?" she asked.

"No. It's less than two hours to home."

"Okay, Conner. Home sounds really good."

"Come on, sunshine. Let's go home then."

Annabel was right by Conner's side as they reached the car. She held Muffin in one arm and reached for her husband's hand with her free hand. Words bubbled up from her heart, and she heard them clearly.

"Love never fails."

This was truth, not confusion.

Annabel had nearly forgotten God, but He hadn't forgotten her. She had been unfaithful to Him and very nearly been unfaithful to Conner. She had put herself and Muffin in danger, but the Lord hadn't left her. She had tried to find the way herself, and it had led down a confusing path of destruction. God, in His great mercy, had saved her from her weakness, pride, and a mistake she would regret for a long time.

She didn't need to reinvent herself. She needed to repent. And trust in Him.

She rested her head against the seat and watched out the window as they headed north. She thought back to her initial drive into the mountains. It felt like weeks had gone by since then, not days. The wheat fields had glowed in the sun as she'd heard fleeting words, *wheat* and *chaff*, largely ignoring them.

Now she understood. Conner was wheat. Jan was chaff. Becoming an artist again was wheat. Trying to do something to gain acceptance was chaff. Most of what she had experienced on this trip to the mountains was merely chaff on the wind. She wanted the winds of God to blow it away forever. She had been given another chance.

This time, she hoped for a harvest that glorified God. The rest was useless chaff.

She sighed and leaned over to take her husband's hand. He glanced at her, smiled, and squeezed her hand.

"What are you smiling about?" Conner asked as he let go and reached his arm around her shoulders.

"Harvest."

"Harvest? That's a strange topic for a city girl."

"City girls eat wheat, too," she said with a giggle.

She was determined no longer to be discontent. She would succeed with her art and not live in fear anymore.

"By the way, just so you know, Muffin is excellent at discernment," she mused.

"Really?" He sounded doubtful. "What makes you say that?"

"She knows the wheat from the chaff."

"The what? Is this a theological chat?"

"I guess it is."

Annabel laughed. Conner chuckled. And Muffin barked.

Study Questions

1. Dreams are significant pathways for God to speak with us. Characters in the Bible had God-given dreams. What dream did Annabel have in this story? What do you think it means? Have you had a vivid dream in which you felt God speaking to you? What was He saying?

2. What were Annabel's special talents or gifts? Which one was she called by God to use? What are your gifts and talents? How can you develop a God-given gift to use as ministry?

3. Was Annabel on the best path in her life? Do you feel you are on the path God has chosen for you?

4. How did Annabel deal with her state of vulnerability? How did Conner deal with it? Name four ways you deal with vulnerable times in your life. Do these strategies keep you safe?

5. Annabel put herself and her beloved dog into potentially dangerous situations that compromised their safety and her ability to feel renewed. Are there choices you have made that put you into harm's way?

6. What was Annabel's biggest challenge? What made it difficult for her to understand it? How did she find answers?

7. Define compromise. How was compromise a factor in Annabel's life? Is there any way that compromise affects your life?

8. Who are the people Annabel met who could negatively affect her walk with God? Are there relationships in your life that could negatively affect your walk with God?

9. Explain Annabel's restlessness and unhappiness. Are there areas of your life where you feel the same?

10. What kept Annabel from using her artistic gifts? Are there things that keep you from using your artistic gifts?

11. Who were Annabel's heroes in this story? Explain. Who are your heroes?

12. What was God's best plan for Annabel's life? What is God's best plan for your life? Spend some time in contemplation and prayer. What comes to mind? What first step could you take to move into that plan?